FLINT 6:
A KING IS BORN

Flint 6:
A KING IS BORN

TREASURE HERNANDEZ

www.urbanbooks.net

Urban Books, LLC
1199 Straight Path
West Babylon, NY 11704

Flint Book 6: A King Is Born © copyright 2009 Treasure Hernandez

ISBN- 13: 978-1-60162-169-6
ISBN- 10: 1-60162-169-8

First Printing November 2009
Printed in the United States of America

10   9   8   7   6   5   4   3

This is a work of fiction. Any references or similarities to actual events, real people, living, or dead, or to real locales are intended to give the novel a sense of reality. Any similarity in other names, characters, places, and incidents is entirely coincidental.

Distributed by Kensington Publishing Corp.
Submit Wholesale Orders to:
Kensington Publishing Corp.
C/O Penguin Group (USA) Inc.
Attention: Order Processing
405 Murray Hill Parkway
East Rutherford, NJ 07073-2316
Phone: 1-800-526-0275
Fax: 1-800-227-9604

FLINT 6:
A KING IS BORN

Prologue

"I want a half-million in seventy-two hours," Mitch said, thinking about all the dough that Malek had exited the drug game with. "If that money isn't in my hands by Friday, you can start picking out Halleigh's casket."

Rare tears filled Malek's eyes. He wasn't sure if they were tears of anger or just feeling so helpless and not in control. How could he have allowed himself to be put into a position where Mitch had the upper hand and was calling the shots?

Malek stood there fighting the emotions of just breaking down in front of his former comrade turned archenemy. But he couldn't do it. He refused to show complete weakness in front of Mitch. It was now obvious that he'd shown his weak side when it came to Halleigh one time too many, which explains why Mitch knew he could get to Malek by kidnapping Halleigh. Not just get to Malek, but

1

get to his money. There was nothing in the world Malek wouldn't do for that girl, and Mitch knew that better than anybody.

Just the thoughts about not being there for his woman when she needed him most cut through Malek's heart like a knife. He was her protector, but he'd gotten so caught up in the paper chase, he had managed to put her in harm's way. Finally, no matter how hard he tried to fight it, Malek's emotions got the best of him as a tear slid down his cheek. He had no idea how he was going to come up with the money Mitch was demanding. He knew that Mitch thought he had money put away; after all, he was the one who had helped put the two million in his retirement fund. But little did Mitch know, Malek was dead broke, since Gary, that con artist, had scammed him out of the entire two million, leaving Malek vowing to get back at him.

Mitch pushed Malek forcefully and smiled. "You better go get my money, bitch," he said as if he were a pimp talking to one of his hoes on a Saturday night. Mitch then motioned his head toward the door, non-verbally dismissing Malek from his sight

Taking his cue, Malek made his exit, with Scratch, his newfound sidekick, following him out of the door. Scratch cared for Halleigh a great deal, so it was unspoken that he'd ride or die with Malek and do whatever to ensure Halleigh's safety. They had three days to get a half-million dollars, which felt next to impossible. But Malek knew that he had to do something to get his love back, and

Scratch was going to do all he could to help. Malek and Scratch exited the house with no plan and little hope.

Halleigh cried her eyes out in the corner of the basement as blood trickled down her leg and her wound ached from being raped by Bugz. The shirt she had on had been ripped, and her eye was beginning to swell because of the blow he delivered to her when she'd tried to resist his advances.

She watched as Bugz exited the room, breathing heavily, a devilish smirk on his face as he finally got a piece of the devil's pie. Once he was no longer in view, Halleigh broke down in a shivering and heaving wail. She grabbed her stomach and cradled it as she worried about her unborn baby that was hopefully still living and growing inside her. She wanted to think positive, but Bugz had done a number on her.

During the sexual assault, she had told Bugz that she was pregnant, but he continued to degrade her without batting an eye. He didn't seem to care at all. In fact, it seemed to excite him and only made him go harder.

Halleigh cried out to Malek as she relived the incident that had just taken place over again in her mind. "Help me, Malek," she whimpered. "Help us." She looked down at her stomach. She then looked around the abandoned room wondering how. Why?

Just when Halleigh had thought her life was changing for the better, the streets of Flint had once again snatched her out of her fairytale. Now she was knee-deep in the game once again. "Help me, God. Help me and my baby," Halleigh cried out, almost in anger after realizing that her pleas for Malek to come rescue her would go unanswered. Now she felt like nobody but God could help her.

Halleigh could feel herself becoming lightheaded and nauseated because of the smell of the semen and blood mixture. She looked down between her legs, and the next thing she knew, a horrendous shriek was bouncing off the cement walls. A shrill resulting from the shock of seeing the blood oozing from between her legs. She could feel herself becoming unconscious and tried her best to stay focused, but that was to no avail. Halleigh began to moan, groan, and grumble some words. The last thing that rolled off her tongue before she blacked out was Malek's name. He had just broken his promise to never let anything else happen to her.

Chapter One

Halleigh's body was racked with violent shivers as she hugged her knees close to her chest and tried to hide herself in the shadows of the dreary basement. She had just come to, having no idea exactly how long she'd been unconscious. For a second there she'd forgotten about what had taken place just moments before she blacked out, but when she looked down at her body, she was quickly reminded.

She looked around the room, her eyes darting from one corner to the next, almost as if she was on drugs, but drugs were a thing of the past. She had been drug-free for a long time. Although no one appeared to be in the room with her, she could feel eyes burning through her.

After a few more moments of scanning the basement, she finally spotted what she could sense was there—the eye of a camera. She could see the tiny red blink of a camcorder in the upper corner of the room. Once again, she felt violated.

She reached out in an attempt to grab something to cover herself, but nothing was there. She had no choice but to resume her earlier position, knees to her chest and her arms curled around her legs as she rocked slowly. A sharp pain forced her to let out a gasp. That's when she recalled that she'd been bleeding ever since Bugz had violated her, and now she feared for her baby's life.

She buried her face between her knees as tears fell from her eyes. She didn't want whoever was watching her to be empowered by her tears, so she felt the need to hide them. She couldn't help but wonder if anybody had been watching her while she was being raped. Who had sat in front of the monitor and witnessed the horrible act without intervening? What type of person could do something like that? Whoever it was, she hated them. Their voyeuristic sin was cruel, and she was desperate for an escape.

Suddenly, Halleigh got a flashback and lifted her head. In the split second between her being snatched from the shower and a cloth being put over her nose and mouth, she'd looked into the bathroom mirror and saw something. Someone. Someone familiar.

"Mitch?" The word fell off her tongue as she realized that all of this was possibly his doing. "I need to see Mitch," she whispered to herself.

If Mitch was behind this entire thing, she knew she had a chance to survive after all. As far as Halleigh knew, she'd never done anything to Mitch to prompt him to do something like this to her, so she could only assume that this had nothing to do with her at all, but everything to do with him and Malek. She didn't know what had sparked a beef between them, but she did know that Mitch had been sweet on her at one point. She was hoping he still was. If so, perhaps she could use it to her advantage. She knew that his attraction toward her was probably the only way she could ever get out of the situation alive, and she was willing to do whatever she had to in order to ensure her baby's safety.

Where are you, Malek? Trembling with fear, her eyes darted frantically around the room. She didn't know what to expect next. It had been a full twenty-four hours since she had been given any food, and she hadn't seen another face besides Bugz's. The thought crossed her mind that, now that Bugz had gotten what he wanted from her and she could identify him, she would be left for dead.

She shook her head in an attempt to erase those dreadful thoughts. She hoped and prayed that Bugz was gone for good, but that someone else would come see about her. Bugz wasn't in this alone; she knew that much. There had to be someone else assigned to keep guard over her, but who? Maybe her eyes had deceived her. Maybe it wasn't Mitch she'd seen before blacking out.

She closed her eyes and ran the scene through her mind. The scene had happened so quickly. She visualized the shadowy figure that stood off to the side, and unless her mind was deceiving her, it was indeed Mitch.

Opening her eyes, Halleigh wished to God this had all been just a bad dream, but the fact remained, she was still being held hostage. The torment of being locked in the basement reminded Halleigh of when Manolo had imprisoned her in his basement for weeks. It had been sheer torture, and she truly believed that a part of her had been forever locked in that basement. When she was finally released, she was a partial image of the person she used to be. She could only wonder what kind of emotions this time would bring upon her. How much of her soul would she leave behind this time, if she made it out at all?

Everything in Halleigh just wanted to get up, go beat on that door, and cry out for help, but she was all out of screams. There was no fight left in her. All she really wanted to do was just go home. She would do anything to be back home, safe and sound in her bed, next to her man.

She closed her eyes once again, and instantly, Malek's face appeared behind her lids. Her heartbeat began to speed up as she thought about the possibility of never seeing him again. She couldn't understand, for the life of her, why it seemed as though the two of them were always teetering on the edge. Why was their love so hard to keep? Just when it appeared as though they'd picked themselves up and dusted themselves off again, they were being kicked back down. Something always seemed to be in their way, keeping them apart.

Halleigh thought, *Perhaps, we're not supposed to be together. True love couldn't possibly be this hard to maintain, could it?*

Tears ran down her face as she kept her eyes squeezed shut. She could see him smiling at her. He was holding her baby—their baby—in his arms. A sob escaped from her lips as she imagined Malek staring lovingly at her, rocking a baby boy back and forth in his arms. Halleigh had never seen that much joy in Malek's face, and she was mesmerized by the child he was holding. He was the most beautiful baby boy she had ever seen. His smooth chocolate skin was flawless, and his big buck eyes were innocent and sweet. She fell in love at first sight, even though it was just a dream.

As quickly as she fell in love, grief took over. She saw Malek fall to his knees with the baby in his hands. His face donned a look of pain, as the front of his white T-shirt filled with crimson blood. Halleigh reached out for him, but she couldn't get to him. She heard her baby crying, but she couldn't move. The only thing she could do was cry.

Halleigh's eyes shot open at the sight of her love dying, and she stared into space. "God, please help us," she pleaded.

She couldn't help but think that her vision was some type of premonition. *That's why he hasn't come for me yet,* she thought. *Please, God, let Malek be okay.* Her love for him was just that deep. Even while she was in distress, she prayed for his well-being. Even if a part of her was angry that he wasn't there for her, she still couldn't help but love him. They were soul mates, and her love for him was unselfish and unyielding. It was evident that, no matter what, she couldn't force herself to not love that man. Only death itself could keep her from loving him. She hoped, though, that wouldn't be the case.

Mitch entered the trap house, his authority causing his henchmen to straighten up and pretend as if they hadn't just been distracted from the game of NBA Live they'd been playing for some hours. Mitch stood in the living room in his Pelle jacket, black hoodie, and Sean John jeans, a Styrofoam food box in his hand. "Turn that bull-shit off," Mitch stated in his low, serious tone. He walked over to the TV monitors and looked at Halleigh on the screen. "She ate?"

Bugz continued to play the game. "Nah."

"Since when?" Mitch pulled his baggy pants up on his waistline.

"Shit, I don't know, man. Yesterday, I think," Bugz replied, refusing to turn his attention away from the game.

"Why not?" Mitch asked calmly as he went over to where Bugz and two other corner boys were sitting.

"The bitch ain't got no act-right in her." Bugz hit the blunt that was being passed around. He chuckled as he thought about his sexual tryst with the captive.

Mitch walked over to the game and snatched the cords out of the wall, interrupting their tournament. "Fuck am I paying you niggas for? Huh? Didn't I give y'all strict or-ders? Why didn't y'all feed her? She's pregnant!"

Bugz frowned and shot back, "Damn, fam! I didn't know we was running a luxury hotel out this bitch. We kid-napped that broad. So I forgot to feed her. I don't see why we hanging onto this bitch anyway. I say we pop her ass and pop that bitch-ass nigga Malek."

Mitch shook his head in disdain and then lunged at Bugz, hemming him up by his collar, and pointing a threatening finger in his face. "You feed her because I say feed her, nigga. I'm boss. You don't need to know why we hanging onto her. I'm not paying you to be sitting around with these mu'fuckas glued to an Xbox. Understand?"

Bugz, embarrassed that he had been degraded in front of his peers, snatched away from Mitch. He humbled himself and replied, "Yeah, I got you, fam." He brushed his shoulders off as if Mitch had gotten dirt on him by touching him. "Damn! My fault, my nigga." Bugz headed toward the kitchen. "I'll go feed her now."

"I got it." Mitch started down the stairs with the food he had for himself, to give it to Halleigh. He mumbled to himself about how incompetent Bugz was as he made his way to the bottom of the steps.

The loud noise his Timberland boots made as he descended the steps sounded identical to Bugz's footsteps, and Halleigh cowered in fear, huddling farther into the corner of the basement.

As Mitch reached the bottom of the steps, he could see her through the darkness. He looked up and fumbled around before he pulled the string hanging from the ceiling to illuminate the room. A yellow glow shone throughout the basement, and a funky smell, like fresh blood, filled the air. Mitch immediately frowned up and walked toward Halleigh. "Halleigh, come and grab some of this food."

Mitch's voice caused her to turn around. "Mitch?" she called out weakly.

He didn't respond.

Halleigh blinked a couple of times, adjusting her eyes to the light. Once she could see clearly, she was able to confirm that she had been right all along. Mitch was the person in the basement with her. He was the second figure she'd seen after being snatched out of the shower.

"Mitch, please let me go. Why are you doing this to me?" she asked from the floor. She wanted to stand, but her body was in too much pain.

Mitch swallowed hard, coaching himself the entire time not to let Halleigh's sweet voice get to him. "Come eat." He squatted down near her and put the food on the floor.

There was a look of terror in Halleigh's eyes, and as guilt bombarded his soul, Mitch tried his best to avoid eye contact with her. It definitely wasn't the same look he'd seen her give Malek, the one he'd secretly longed for. The last thing he ever wanted was for her to look at him as a monster, the way she was now.

As Mitch looked downward, dodging Halleigh's eyes, he noticed dried blood between her thighs. He could smell sex and sweat in the air. He frowned as he lifted her chin and rubbed her hair gently, as if she was his woman.

Halleigh closed her eyes. She couldn't stand to look into his eyes like that. She could still feel him staring at her, though. She began to shake, thinking that he, too, would force himself on her.

Mitch observed the torn shirt as well. Between that, the blood, and the smell, he put two and two together in his mind. Mitch's hands began to shake. His eyes scanned Halleigh once more. Her once confident swagger was replaced with fear and an insecurity he hadn't seen in her since her days as a Manolo Mami.

Mitch thought about his hardheaded worker. *No wonder Bugz hadn't fed her. He was too busy trying to fuck her. Son of a bitch!*

"Mitch, please, " Halleigh whispered, interrupting his

thoughts, "I need to see a doctor. He raped me, Mitch. He hurt me real bad. I just need to make sure my baby is okay. That's all I want to do. Please, Mitch."

Too pissed for Halleigh's soft words to even penetrate him at that moment, Mitch clenched his jaw and rose to his feet. He emerged from the basement and stood near the door as he motioned for Bugz to approach him.

"Yeah, uh, what's up, fam?" Bugz stammered. He could tell by the menacing look on Mitch's face that Mitch wasn't too pleased with him. He'd already gotten on him about starving the poor girl, so certainly he was over that and on to something else.

Mitch stared Bugz straight in the eyes, daring him to try to lie. "Why is she bleeding?"

Bugz attempted to laugh the tension away. "I told you the bitch ain't got no act-right, so a nigga had to put some up in her." He snatched at his crotch and turned to walk away.

Mitch called out to one of the other henchmen sitting on the couch. "Yo, Jake."

"What up?" Jake replied.

BOOM!

Out of nowhere, Mitch put a bullet through the back of Bugz's head. "Clean this mu'fucka up." Mitch glared from one corner boy to the other. The room was quiet. "Any of you other niggas who can't follow orders gon' find yourself in the same predicament. I said watch her and feed her, nothing more, nothing less."

Jake hopped up and did as he was told. He shook his head in shock as he began to dispose of the body, but he didn't dare say a word. He wasn't trying to see Mitch, and he definitely wasn't trying to be next.

Just as quickly as Mitch's temper had flared, it settled, and he went back into the basement. He removed the coat he was wearing and covered Halleigh's body before picking her up and carrying her up the stairs.

Halleigh, her body limp in Mitch's arms, almost like a rag doll, hadn't the slightest idea where Mitch could be taking her, but she didn't even have the energy to protest anyway. Being in a damp basement, she knew whatever he had in store for her couldn't be worse than that. Besides, Mitch's arms provided her with warmth from his body heat.

The first thing Halleigh saw when she emerged from the basement in Mitch's arms was Bugz's dead body on the floor. She looked up at Mitch, who simply stepped over the body without a word then carried her up another flight of stairs. He took her to a bedroom and laid her on the queen-size bed.

"Look, Halleigh, this wasn't supposed to happen," Mitch finally spoke. "This wasn't part of the plan."

"Plan?" Halleigh asked, a puzzled look on her face. "What plan, Mitch? What's going on?"

Refusing to allow the tenderness in Halleigh's voice to get to him, Mitch ignored her queries. "I'ma call a friend of mine over here to check on you and make sure you and your baby are okay." He deliberately put some sternness into his voice to let Halleigh know that, even though he was about to get her some help, he still meant business. "Don't act a fucking fool up in here either, screaming and all that. Don't give me a reason to hurt you, Halleigh. I don't want to take it there with you, so don't leave me without a choice. Just chill out for a minute, and at the end of all this, you will walk out of here unharmed."

Halleigh shook her head in disgust. "I don't understand you, Mitch," she replied, her voice laced with hatred. Confused, hurt, and mad, Halleigh needed to get to the bottom of this and find out what was going on. Why would Mitch be doing this to his best friend's woman? "You were Malek's friend. He trusted you. I trusted you, Mitch. Why would you do this to us? Is this about you and me? I mean, I'm not blind. I've noticed the subtle ways you are with me. And, believe me, Mitch, you are a good guy, but . . . I could never be with you."

Mitch laughed charmingly, rubbing his neatly trimmed goatee. He shook his head in disagreement. He gently rubbed the back of his hand across Halleigh's cheek. "It was good, ma, but it wasn't that good." He pulled his hand away. "I don't beef out over no broad, but let me put it to you like this: Maybe if you had chosen differently, you wouldn't be in this situation. This shit don't happen to niggas like me. Only niggas like Malek. He ain't a gangster; he's a ballplayer. He should've stuck to the game he knew best. Believe it or not, he started this war. Now I'ma finish that nigga."

Mitch walked over to the door. Before exiting the room, he turned to Halleigh and said, "Now I'ma have my niggas set up the cameras in this room. The windows are armorguarded, and the door has a dead bolt. Don't be stupid, which means, don't try anything stupid." Mitch turned to leave, but then he walked back over to Halleigh. "Oh, yeah, and don't even bother wasting your time thinking about Malek. That nigga is as good as dead."

He looked down at Halleigh's stomach. "I suggest you better concentrate on keeping you and yours alive." Mitch reached to stroke Halleigh's face, but she smacked his hand away forcefully. He smiled. He couldn't help but admire her loyalty. He had known all along that her loyalty to Malek was stopping him from pursuing her, which was why he never really stepped to her like he wanted to. He knew it would be in vain, as long as Malek was still around. Mitch knew that Halleigh would never choose him, even after Malek's death. She loved that boy way too much, and although he didn't like it, he respected it. Any nigga in the game would have loved to have a for-real ride-or-die chick like Halleigh on their team.

Unfortunately, she'd never be on his, especially not now. With that final thought, Malek turned around and walked out, leaving her alone.

Although she'd managed to maintain her composure while Mitch spat all that venom about Malek her way, now that he was out of sight, she began to cry her eyes out. Although he had basically promised her she would be okay, he had also assured her that Malek was going to die. If that was the case, she didn't even care anymore whether she lived. She couldn't see herself living without Malek. *What am I going to do?*

She could feel herself hyperventilating. With each forced breath, her heart hurt tremendously. She could feel the pit of emptiness expanding in her stomach. She wanted to scream for help, but knew better than to test Mitch. Still, she couldn't just sit there, knowing that her baby's father was about to be introduced to death. She had to do something. She had to make a move. Everyone else seemed to have a plan; now it was time for her to come up with one of her own.

Chapter Two

Malek breathed heavily, and his palms began to sweat profusely. He watched closely as the other people in the bank casually tended to their business unaware of what was in store for them. He tried to look composed as he began to fill out a deposit slip under a fake name. He took a deep breath and thought, *It's all or nothing.*

With that simple thought, he erased any hesitation that dwelled in his heart. He couldn't turn back. Halleigh's survival and that of the child she was carrying in her womb depended on it.

Malek looked around, inconspicuously casing the place. The bank was small, but under heavy surveillance. Malek had scoped out the cameras in each corner of the lobby and also those pointed directly at the tellers' drawers.

Malek glanced at the middle-aged white security guard who stood in the corner. He noted the overzealous look in the security guard's eyes, as if he'd been on the job for so many years just waiting for something to jump off. He wasn't just a flashlight security guard either. Medium-built, and most likely a police officer moonlighting, this guy had a black .45 on his hip and patted it every so often, to make sure it was there.

Malek knew the security guard wanted to be a hero, and was just waiting for the opportunity to pull that gun from the holster and shoot it. If anything went wrong with his plan, the guard would be a problem.

Malek knew he was taking penitentiary chances by sticking up a bank, but the only thing on his mind was getting Halleigh's ransom. He clenched his jaws and gripped the pen tightly as he thought about Halleigh probably being tied up somewhere, hoping he would come for her, or even worse, giving up on him completely for not being there to prevent it all from happening in the first place.

Malek's eyes began to water. He had failed in his responsibility to protect Halleigh and his unborn child. And this wasn't even the first time he'd failed her. The guilt felt like a ton of bricks on his shoulders. What type of husband and father would he make if he couldn't keep his family safe?

The fact that Mitch had taken his most prized possession had Malek questioning his manhood. *How could I have let this happen?*

He glanced at the door as Scratch, acting drunk off his

ass, stumbled into the bank. In actuality, Scratch was as sober as a preacher on Easter, so his demeanor was all a part of their plan. Scratch was to cause a distraction and draw the attention of the security guard, while Malek robbed the place. As long as Scratch stayed in character, Malek felt like it was all a sure thing.

Scratch was staggering and talking loud, a brown paper bag in his hand. At first sight, you'd think it was a forty-ounce beer bottle in the bag, but Scratch, prepared to shoot, just in case he needed to clear a way for them to exit, already had his finger wrapped around the trigger of the pistol inside.

The guard, patting that damn gun as if it were a magnet and his hand was metal, kept a watchful eye on the bank's patrons. Just as planned, he immediately motioned toward Scratch.

That's when Malek, his fitted cap pulled low over his eyes and exposing only the bottom portion of his face, headed to the first open teller in sight. He took a deep breath and walked to the teller, whose eyes were focused on the ruckus by the bank's entrance.

"Where in the hell is the manager?" Scratch yelled.

By now everyone in the bank was looking at Scratch, standing in the middle of the lobby, swaying back and forth as if he couldn't keep his balance.

"My damn ATM card just got stuck, and I want my damn money!" he yelled. "I'm almost out of my drinky-drinky, and I needs my money to get some more."

While Scratch played his part to the nines, Malek approached the female bank teller. He was so high on his own adrenaline, he felt as if he would throw up, but he still pushed forward. Malek reached into his hoodie pocket and slowly placed the chrome .45 on the counter, his finger on the trigger.

Finally pulling her attention away from Scratch, the teller attempted to greet Malek. "How are you to—" She stopped mid-sentence after she glanced down and noticed the pistol pointed directly at her midsection. She flinched and put her hand on her chest. "Oh my God," she whispered, her breathing becoming shallow.

"Just relax and keep your cool," Malek instructed in a low tone. "You know what time it is." Then he added in the most subtle voice he could muster, "And if you try anything funny, I'ma have to push yo' shit back. Okay?"

The teller simply nodded her head in fear. Too afraid to do anything other than that, she stared down at the gun, praying and hoping it stayed right there in its place.

"Now, I want you to give me the unmarked bills in your drawer. Put them in that big envelope right there." Malek pointed to a money deposit envelope among the many stored behind the teller, the type of leather pouch businesses use to make deposits. "Give me all hundreds and fifties, ma." He cocked the gun. "And if you even think about triggering the silent alarm, I'm going to make sure you're the first person I kill before the police get here."

Once again, all the teary-eyed teller could do was nod, her chest rising up and down. Malek could clearly hear her inhaling and exhaling.

Malek noticed the pictures of the teller and her children placed inside her space. "Give me the money, so you can go home to your kids. Now, just calm down and be smart," Malek said, trying to coach her through the robbery.

She fought back her tears, doing just as Malek had instructed.

"You're doing good." Malek briefly looked over his shoulder to make sure Scratch still had the guard's full attention.

Scratch almost came to blows with the security guard and was being pushed out of the bank.

"Get yo' mu'fuckin' hands off me, man!"

Scratch tried to get back into the bank, but the burly guard wasn't having it. Scratch was putting up a hell of a fight and causing a scene, but the security guard was too big for him to muscle through. Even the bank manager had approached them.

With all of this going on, not one person was paying attention to Malek and the teller.

After tangling with Scratch for another minute or so, the guard finally decided to just pick Scratch up and toss him out of the building like Mr. Banks used to do to Jazzy Jeff on *The Fresh Prince of Bel-Air*.

Just as Scratch was hitting the ground, Malek was coming out of the building, the bank deposit pouch stuffed with money under his armpit, inside his coat. He even smiled at the guard on his way out.

Scratch got up from the ground, fussing and cussing all the way around the corner. He was sure enough putting on a scene, until he rounded the corner, flipping the security guard the bird as he walked out of sight, to where Malek was waiting on him in the parked car.

"Let's go, Scratch!" Malek yelled out of the window as he started up the car.

Scratch hurried into the waiting vehicle, and they sped off without looking back.

Before the guard even noticed that the bank had just been robbed, Malek and Scratch were gone. Malek thanked God that he had gotten out of the bank without falter. Locked up, he would be no good to anyone. He had just taken a major risk.

Even so, he knew that the bank envelope didn't hold all the ransom money he needed to get Halleigh back. So, as he drove, he tried to get his mental together, preparing for bank job number two.

Just minutes later, Malek and Scratch were at another bank not too far from the one they'd just robbed. Working with very little time, they couldn't afford to take a break. They had to do this thing guerilla-style. He had to go all out to get the half-million.

Malek and Scratch tried to run the same game that had worked so well at the first bank, but this time they ran into a problem: a cop came in during the middle of their caper.

When he'd arrived at the bank, Malek had filled out a deposit slip, the same as before. He scoped the place out and noticed the security guard to be less alert than the one at the bank he'd just robbed. He was too busy checking out the females' asses to pay attention to Malek. The more Malek thought about it, he probably really didn't even need Scratch to perform his Oscar-winning role. The big-booty women were distraction enough. Still, if it wasn't broke, there was no need to fix it, so things went on as planned.

Ironically, though, a cop came to the bank on his lunch break to cash his Friday paycheck. Just as he pulled up in front of the bank and was about to get out of his car, he heard on his police scanner about the bank robbery that had just taken place. He listened as the voice on the radio explained the manner of the robbery, one man causing a distraction while another man stuck up a teller.

At first he was going to drive over to the other bank location to see if they needed any assistance, but confident that his fellow officers had everything under control, he decided that since he was already at the bank, he'd go ahead and cash his check and stop by the other bank afterward.

When the police officer got out of his car and entered the bank, he walked in and saw Scratch acting a fool. The security guard on duty was almost unable to contain the man. The officer shook his head, realizing that this security guard probably needed his help more than the officers down at the other bank.

"Where the damn manager?" Scratch yelled. "My fuckin' money didn't come out that raggedy-ass ATM machine." He walked over to the banker's desk in the middle of the medium-sized bank.

Malek was taking the money from the teller, while the

security guard was trying to calm Scratch. Just like before, all eyes were on Scratch.

Except the police officer who'd just entered the bank.

At first, it was the officer's instincts to go over and try to help get the situation under control, but then he remembered the call that came over the radio describing the technique used to rob the bank earlier.

He looked around, wondering what the chances were of the same exact thing taking place just a few blocks away a few moments later. When he saw Malek and the teller—the only two people in the bank not distracted by the commotion going on between Scratch and the security guard—he knew the chances were greater than he'd initially assumed.

The police officer slipped his hand down to his gun and walked up behind Malek.

"Remember, just stay calm and everything will be okay," Malek reminded the nervous teller. He tried to keep his head low, his fitted cap yet again covering most of his eyes. He could see the teller slipping one hand under the counter as she gave him the money with her other hand. "What the fuck you think you doing?" Malek said in a harsh whisper. He pulled back the hammer on his gun, which lay on the counter pointed toward her.

She quickly put her hands where Malek could see them.

Before he could do anything else, he heard the voice of the police officer behind him.

"Put your hands in the air where I can see them, son," the officer ordered, his gun aimed at Malek. "It's over.

You're not getting out of here with this money today," the officer said sternly, but without raising his voice.

The cop deliberately used a calm tone because he didn't know Malek's state of mind and didn't want his suspect to harm the innocent teller, who was already visibly frightened.

"Fuck!" Malek cursed to himself under his breath as he thought quickly about what to do. But what could he do with a gun pointed to his head? Still, that didn't keep his mind from racing for a way out—hopefully, with the money.

Within five seconds, Malek had weighed his options and decided to do what he had to do. "I'm not going to jail today," he whispered. He swung around, catching the unsuspecting cop off guard with his bold actions, and immediately began firing his gun, hitting the cop in the midsection.

The cop managed to let off a couple of rounds, but none of them hit Malek, who ducked, dipped, and dodged toward the exit, using people as live body shields to deter the cop from firing at him for fear of shooting an innocent bystander.

Immediately, the patrons in the bank went into a frenzy at the sound of the gunfire, and the eerie screams of a stampede caused by the panic echoed throughout the building.

Before the security guard could react, Scratch had grabbed the guard's gun from his waist and pointed it at him.

Malek saw the officer he'd shot gasping for air as he

dropped his gun and held his midsection. "Damn, damn, damn!" Malek repeated, as it registered in his brain that he'd just shot a cop.

Malek quickly exited the bank, and Scratch followed close behind, almost out of breath.

"What the fuck happened, youngblood?" Scratch's eyes were bigger than golf balls. He couldn't believe what had just gone down. It was a horrible misstep that was sure to make them wanted men, especially if the cop died.

The Flint Police Department was like a gang in its own right. When one of their own went down, they showed no mercy on the transgressor. Malek and Scratch would be hunted to no end, and when, or if, they were caught, they might not ever make it to the jailhouse. The Flint police might just deliver them to their graves.

"We weren't supposed to kill nobody. That was a fuckin' jake!" Scratch yelled as they hopped in the car.

Malek quickly sped off. His mind was so messed up over the shooting, he didn't even stop to to see if there were any cars coming, and almost hit a passing car as he pulled off.

As they weaved in and out of traffic, Scratch cautioned, "Watch it, youngblood."

"My fault." Malek looked through his rearview mirror to make sure they weren't being followed. He hit the steering wheel with his fist. "He just ran up on me, man," Malek yelled as he maneuvered through traffic and made the getaway. "I had to."

Scratch kept looking back to see if anyone was behind

them as they sped away, trying to get as far away from the scene of the crime as possible.

Malek periodically looked in his rearview and then focused back on the road. "Fuck!" he yelled again, repeatedly hitting the steering wheel.

Once again he peeked in his rearview and then looked at Scratch, who looked more nervous than ever. They had just stepped into the big leagues. Not only were they bank robbers, but possible cop killers.

Chapter Three

Halleigh cringed at the touch of the skinny white man Mitch had called over to check on her condition. Halleigh didn't know the man, nor was he dressed in a white coat, but Mitch kept referring to him as Doc, so she assumed he was some street doctor they used in the game whenever one of their crew members got hurt or something.

Halleigh felt very uncomfortable as this stranger examined the most intimate parts her body, especially with Mitch standing there watching the entire thing. At first Halleigh kept her eyes shut tight, to keep from seeing him standing there, but then she thought maybe if she did make eye contact with him, he would help her out a little.

Halleigh tried to look in Mitch's eyes, hoping that his conscience would get the better of him and he would find it in his heart to let her go. But every time she tried to lock eyes with him, he would just look away and avoid eye contact with her altogether.

After a brief exam that took all of five minutes, Doc put his stethoscope and other tools inside his small gray leather bag and stood up. "Mitch, she should be fine. She just needs some rest." Doc dug down into his leather bag and handed Mitch a bottle of pills. "And have her take a couple of these aspirin. She'll be okay."

Doc also avoided eye contact with Halleigh and never spoke to her directly, just to Mitch. He walked toward the door, where Mitch was standing, and then glanced back at Halleigh. He leaned in close to Mitch and whispered, "What do you guys have going on here?"

"Get the fuck outta here." Mitch grabbed Doc by the collar and escorted him out the door. "Jake will pay you on your way out," he said, as the doctor hurried down the stairs.

Mitch returned to the room and focused back on Halleigh, who was balled into a fetal position. For a brief moment, he wondered if he'd done the right thing, using her to get to Malek, putting her in the middle of a street beef, when in reality she had nothing to do with the matter. Nevertheless, his pride wouldn't allow him to admit that he was wrong, nor allow him to punk out and give Malek the win by letting Halleigh go without collecting a ransom.

"It's all just a part of the game," he whispered to himself, trying to ease the guilt that rested square on his shoulders. He walked over to Halleigh and tossed the bottle on the foot of the bed. He began to say something to her, to let her know that everything was going to be all right, but he couldn't think of any words to say. So, he didn't say anything at all. He just turned and left the room, not even offering her a glass of water to take her pills.

Halleigh heard the sound of the door closing, followed soon after by the clicking noises of the locks being turned. She glanced at the camera that Mitch had made one of his goons put in the high corner of the room, and gave the middle finger to whoever was watching her. Although she could be the sweetest, most loving and forgiving person in the world, right now Halleigh was full of nothing but pure hatred, and the object of her emotions was none other than Mitch. She hated Mitch with a deep passion.

Everything in her wished that she could kill him, but she wasn't a killer. She never had been and knew that she never would be. It just wasn't in her. But if ever she just snapped and lost her mind, Mitch would definitely be at the top of the list of all the people who'd hurt her in her life.

It was almost as if Mitch could feel the daggers of hate being shot at him by Halleigh. He'd tried to get her off of his mind by blasting his car stereo with Lil' Wayne's latest, but as he cruised down North Saginaw Street, his thoughts kept going back and forth to Halleigh being left locked up back at the spot. Something in him was urging him to go back to the spot and let her go free. "Fuck that! That nigga Malek gon' feel pain," he said, trying to justify what he was doing to Halleigh.

He hit his steering wheel out of frustration as he

jumped on the highway to go over to Keesha's house. If anything could get his mind off his wrongdoings, it was Keesha's head game.

A few minutes later, Mitch pulled into Howard Estates apartment complex, where Keesha lived, and parked his Land Rover in the handicap space. He checked his mirrors and his surroundings before he got out of the car to enter the building. He patted his hip to make sure he was strapped. After scoping the scene for a couple of seconds, he hopped out.

When he made it to Keesha's door, he noticed that it was slightly cracked. His antenna immediately went up, because he had taught Keesha to always keep her doors locked and closed, no matter what.

Mitch slowly pulled out his gun and crept into the apartment. Keesha's spot was a place he frequented, to get a shot of pussy from time to time. Anyone who knew Mitch knew this about him. They didn't have to hire a private investigator or anything to follow his trail to Keesha's. Keeping that in mind, he wondered if someone, perhaps someone like Malek, was inside waiting for him.

At that moment he wished he'd gone with his first instinct to put one of his boys on Malek, to watch him just as closely as his boys had been watching Halleigh. That way he could be sure of every move Malek was trying to make, just to make sure he didn't try something stupid. But it was too little too late for all that.

Mitch slowly crept through the door, his gun cocked and loaded. He heard the sound from the television com-

Chapter Four

Malek's eyes were red ___ ___ without sleep. There was no way he co___ ___ until he had Halleigh back. In deep concentra___ ___ sat silently, his elbows on his knees, and his ___ ___ clasped together and propped underneath h___ ___.

Unsu___ ___ what to say, Scratch sat nearby staring at Malek ___ He, too, had next to no rest as he and Malek thought of w___ys to get Halleigh from Mitch's clutches. With the sh___oting of the cop on their hands, their chances of getti___g away with another bank robbery were slim to none.

For the past couple of hours, Malek had been racking his brain while Scratch sat there in silence, not wanting to interrupt him. Fresh out of ideas, Scratch knew it was best that he just remain quiet if he wasn't coming up with a plan to make some money to get Halleigh.

With not a word spoken in the last couple of hours, it

was obvious that both Malek and Scratch were at a loss. Scratch had a bad feeling about the entire situation. He knew that the amount of money that Mitch was requesting for Halleigh's ransom was damn near impossible to acquire in such a short period of time. Back in the day, if a man demanded an outrageous ransom then, nine times out of ten, he never really had any intention of giving the kidnap victim back anyway. Scratch hoped and prayed that this wasn't the case and made sure not to let Malek on to his theory.

Malek felt Scratch's eyes on him. "What?" he asked.

Scratch simply cast his eyes downward, hoping that Malek couldn't look into them and read his mind.

"I know what you're thinking, man, but don't say it. I can't deal with that right now." Malek let out a sigh and wiped his hands down his face. "I promise that if Halleigh doesn't come out of this, I'm not going to be able to live, man." He shook his head in despair. "I can't live without her. I tried that before, and it doesn't work. Without Hal, there's no point in me being here, so she has to come out of this. She has to."

Scratch wasn't so sure himself, but he tried to assure his friend. He knew he needed to be the voice of reason right now. "She will. If she can survive years on the street with a cold-blooded muthafucka like Manolo, then she should be able to get through this. Halleigh's a smart girl. I'm sure she's playing the hand she was dealt, but still, we've got to get to her quick. There's only fifty-two cards in a deck, if you know what I'm saying."

"I feel you, but I'm not going to try to kid myself. A half-mil in seventy-two hours? We were pretty much doomed from the start." Malek stood up and began pacing. "Perhaps we went about this all wrong in the first place. Instead of wasting time running up in banks, trying to get that paper, we should have been running up on Mitch's bitch ass."

Scratch had to "lightweight" agree with him, but it was too late for all that now. They had to come up with something else. "You've got to think, youngblood. There's got to be a way for us to get to Halleigh besides coming through with that ransom." Scratch looked at Malek. "You know Mitch. He was your right hand for a minute there. You know what makes him tick. You know what makes him soft. Whichever button we push, we need for him to be off his square. Everybody slips up every now and then. It's just a matter of getting caught. So what it boils down to is that we need to catch that nigga slippin', plain and simple as that." Scratch spoke with so much confidence, the impossible now sounded possible.

Malek absorbed what Scratch was saying and realized he was right. He knew Mitch the same way Mitch knew him. The same way Mitch knew how to get at him, he could turn the tables and do the same with Mitch.

No longer pacing, Malek stood erect with confidence. *I put this nigga in the position that he's in now,* he thought. *The same way I put him in the game, I'ma have to take his ass out.*

Malek couldn't take on the streets by himself, not even with old faithful Scratch by his side. Mitch had the allegiance of most hoods in Flint because he allowed anyone to eat, no matter what side of the city they were from. He had united the North and South Sides. And although Malek had love and respect in the streets, he couldn't fuck with niggas that weren't from his side of the tracks.

Sweets and the South Side would never come up on Malek's watch, which was why he was now at a disadvantage. He needed more players on his team. *I can do this, but I need help,* he reasoned. *I can't put Halleigh at risk by trying to be on some Rambo-type shit. If I make a wrong step, then she could get hurt. I can't jeopardize her like that. I've jeopardized her safety enough already. This shit is bigger than me and my ego. I have to think about her and my seed.*

"So," Scratch started after watching the invisible wheels in Malek's head churn, "what are we going to do, youngblood? 'Cause Scratch'll go out blazing to save Li'l Rina. So you just say the word and tell me the plan."

Malek shot Scratch a serious look before taking a seat. "We're going to rob Mitch!" he said, his voice low and his eyes focused as if deep in thought. "That's our only choice. He's the only person getting money like that in the city. Even if we hit another bank, it won't produce enough money. Besides, you know every bank in town is on lock right about now. We need to hit Mitch's stash spot. Fuck it! This mu'fucka want a half a million, then I'm gonna rob him and pay him back with his own paper. It's our only way to get Hal back."

"Okay, okay! Now you thinking, youngblood," Scratch replied as he stood and began to pace the room. He didn't pace the floor out of nervousness or worry. He was pacing out of anxiousness. He couldn't wait to set it off. The thrill of the game had for certain crept back into Scratch's heart as a smile crossed his face, showing off his crooked, yellow teeth. "By hook or crook we gonna bring baby girl home," Scratch declared. "But there's only one problem that I can think of." Scratch stopped pacing and looked at Malek. "Now, I ain't been in the game in a good while, but the game don't change. I know Mitch ain't the big man. He's running the city, but he don't own no boats. He's getting his product from somewhere. If we rob Mitch, then we might potentially catch heat from his connect."

"Then we'll go to his connect. I put Mitch on. I know Fredro through Jamaica Joe. I'm a man and I stand on my own two, but I'll do anything to get Halleigh back safely. If I got to get at Fredro to get at Mitch, then so be it. But hopefully we can avoid any excess drama if I can just call in a favor." Malek then added, "Fredro was close to Joe, so I hope he's willing to lend me a hand." Malek stood to his feet and walked out of the room. Before he stepped out of view, he said, "If Fredro becomes a problem, then he can get it too."

"Hold up now, youngblood. I hear you, and I'm trying to save Halleigh too, but this is a suicide mission. Our two guns can't go up against Fredro. Just think about it."

Malek nodded his head, let out a sigh, and then whispered, "You're right, but I've got to figure out what to do before it's too late."

Scratch just shook his head and shrugged his shoulders as he sat down to think. He didn't have a clue either, and although just a minute ago he was pumped up, he felt in his bones that this thing wasn't going to end well.

He walked over to the mirror and straightened out his

crumpled clothes, popping his collar. He looked at the bruises and bloody lip that Mitch's goons had caused him and said, "That young boy Mitch got a thing or two coming, if he thinks he can fuck with good ol' Scratch and get away with it." Scratch turned from side to side, examining his profile. "We're going to get you back, Hal."

When Malek returned to the room, Scratch turned to him and said, "First thing we need to do is count up this money and see how much more we need to come up with."

That thought hadn't even crossed Malek's mind. He and Scratch began to count out the money from the two bank robberies combined.

"This is only fifty-two thousand, and we done hit two banks," Malek barked. "How do this nigga expect me to come up with five hundred thousand in three days? That shit is impossible, and he knows it." Malek noticed his hands shaking. He picked up a stack of money and threw it back down on the table.

He didn't want to think about what Mitch would do to Halleigh if he didn't come through with the ransom. Mitch had never had anything against Halleigh, as far as Malek could tell, but that didn't mean he wouldn't do something bad to her to get back at him. After all, Malek had made Mitch look like a bitch-ass nigga in front of Keesha, so it really didn't surprise him that Mitch would want to make him look the same in front of Halleigh. *Perhaps that's all he wants to do is to make me look bad in front of Halleigh.* It was possible that Mitch never had any intention of hurting

Halleigh at all. Maybe all he wanted was to just strip Malek down to nothing by getting him for all of his money.

Mitch probably thought that Malek was sitting on major dough, but the reality was, he was dead broke. Malek's stupidity and naiveté had gotten him swindled and left his pockets on *E*. He was back where he had begun—at the bottom—but the only difference was, he didn't have Jamaica Joe to lean on. Now his right hand was an ex-junkie, a far cry from the powerful reach of Joe.

Malek was grateful for Scratch rolling with him. Besides, he couldn't be choosy. Not a lot of people would rock with him right now, so he had to be grateful for Scratch's loyalty. He didn't know why Scratch was so loyal to Halleigh, but he appreciated it and began to respect Scratch and Halleigh's friendship.

Malek looked over at Scratch, who now appeared to have a worried look in his eyes. Malek could sense his pain.

Scratch looked up when he felt Malek looking at him. "This some bullshit, youngblood. We gotta get Li'l Rina back. This shit ain't fo' her, man. It ain't for her. She don't deserve any mess like this. The game done gone stone crazy. All you young ones don't know a thing about it. Women and children used to be off limits. Now you dummies are snatching 'em off the street as if they are the ones responsible for the chaos." Scratch shook his head and ran his fingers through his matted 'fro. He then sat back and began to think of all the avenues of getting money. "This robbing banks shit ain't gon' cut it. We need to hit hustlers. That way, we don't have to worry about no police heat. If we hit a nigga in the game, what he gon' do? Run to the police screaming that someone ran in his spot and stole his drug money?"

There was a brief silence as Scratch looked to Malek for a response. The look on Malek's face let Scratch know he was making sense. "Exactly, youngblood," Scratch replied to Malek's non-verbal response.

"That's what I've been on, but it's only one person I'm trying to see right now and that's Mitch." Malek slowly nodded his head up and down, agreeing with his own statement.

"What about that Fredro fella you was talking about earlier?" Scratch asked. "We go against Mitch, we might as well sign our own death certificates, because them Italians don't play."

"Dominican," Malek corrected.

"Italian, Dominican, Swiss and cheddar . . . whatever—you know what I'm saying, youngblood. We mess with Mitch's money, we gonna catch heat. Now, don't get me wrong. Scratch ain't no punk. I don't mind any heat it may bring. I'm willing to go all out, but you got to know what you are jumping into before you even take that first leap."

Malek was desperate, and although he knew Scratch had a point, he didn't see any other options. "Fuck it! Like I said before, if Fredro got a problem, then he can get it too," Malek said, putting all the pieces in place as if he were playing chess.

"We gonna rob that boy and pay him with his own paper, huh?" Scratch repeated more to himself than to Malek. He began to chuckle and nodded his head. "I'm in! We have to move fast though, ya dig?" Scratch sat up, leaned in over the table, and began to put together a plan as the seconds ticked by. "Yeah, yeah! We can hit Mitch's spots and give him his own money before word get back to him that his trap spots have been hit. We can get Li'l Rina back that way."

Malek didn't think the idea was the smartest way to go about things, but with only a day left to get the money, it seemed like the only option. "Mitch isn't dumb," Malek said, trying to look at the plan from every angle. "He probably changed up the whole operation since I left. I know he doesn't keep the money in the same spot that we used to. We have no way of finding out the main spot where the dough is. That shit isn't as easy as it seems, old man, and if I know anything about Mitch, it's that he ain't a stupid nigga."

"Well, in my world, nothing is a secret. In the smack-uscr circle, everybody knows something. Maybe we need to ask around and see what we can come up with. It might not seem like it, but users have their own little community, ya dig?" Scratch stood up. "Take Scratch to his old stomping ground and let's see what we can come up with."

Chapter Five

Malek held his nose as he followed Scratch through a walkway and under the overpass of the highway. The stench was horrendous, and the smell of blood and body odor was overwhelming. The Michigan snow didn't hit under the overpass as it did the rest of the city, so it became the safe haven for the city's underworld. There, bums and users, with their cardboard-box houses, huddled around barrels of fire, trying to stay warm.

As Scratch made his way toward the back, he was being greeted left and right, like a hobo superstar. Scratch's popularity reminded Malek of his own, back in his days of walking the hall at his old high school. Malek couldn't help but smile as he watched Scratch do his signature pimp walk through the slum. Not only was Scratch respected amongst the homeless, he was like their mayor.

Malek was surprised at how influential Scratch really was, and how much he knew the ins and outs of the drug game in Flint. No wonder Joe had trusted him to be his eyes and ears on the street. Scratch was privy to stuff that even Joe's own crew didn't know.

Malek made a mental note. He would look at crack-heads and junkies in a new light. He would no longer demean them, because through his interactions with Scratch, he realized they were people too. They were just fucked up and forgotten, but they were also valuable.

Scratch looked around. For some reason, he felt uncomfortable. He had never been sober while living on the streets, and for the first time, he was embarrassed about the lifestyle he used to lead. Scratch, because of his twelve-step program, hadn't been to the spot in months. He'd even promised himself never to revisit the place, but he felt this situation was worth breaking his vow. Halleigh was worth more to him than anyone else in the world. She'd seen through his exterior and began to appreciate the person he was inside, and for that, he would always love her and would die trying to save her. They were friends and so much more.

Malek leaned in close to Scratch and whispered, "Who are we looking for?"

"We need to see Grady." Scratch continued to scan the surroundings. "Good ol' dirty-ass Grady. He's one stinky-ass muthafucka, but he knows everybody and everything that goes down on the north side of Flint. You think Scratch see all, hear all, and know all when it comes to the streets? Scratch ain't got nothing on Grady."

Scratch spotted Stuttering Ron huddled over a barrel of fire and dressed in raggedy clothes and a holy skullcap. "Yo, Ron!" he yelled, getting the homeless man's attention.

"Yo, Scratch! Wha-wha-what's happening, baby!" Ron headed over toward Scratch and Malek.

Scratch leaned into Malek and quickly whispered, "Watch yo' pockets around this nigga, youngblood. He will steal yo' drawers off yo' ass, without you even knowing that they're gone until you go to pull them up after taking a piss."

Malek chuckled and watched as Ron approached them.

Scratch and Ron shook hands and hugged as they reunited. Scratch was happy to see Ron still hanging in there. He and Stuttering Ron used to get high together in that same area, where Scratch had watched many men get taken by Ron without even realizing it. He might have been strung out, but his pickpocketing skills were comparable to none. His hands were quick, and his tongue even quicker. And because he had nothing to lose, there was no one he wouldn't try to sheist.

"W-w-where you been at? We missed you 'r-round here. And who this green nigga you got with you?" Ron immediately recognized that Malek wasn't a user. A seasoned user could always tell when they weren't amongst their own kind.

Scratch glanced over at Malek, whose jaws tightened at the comment the junkie had just made. "Aw, he cool, man. This my potna." Scratch threw his head toward Malek.

Once Scratch vouched for Malek, he was good. Ron reached out his hand to greet Malek. "What's happening, my man?"

Malek looked at Ron like he was crazy and left his hand hanging in the air.

Scratch interjected and began to work his mouthpiece in order to try to locate Grady. "Yo, where is Grady? I need to ask him a few things."

"He's over there catching a nod." Ron pointed to the far corner where a man was sitting down propped up against the wall.

Ron gave Scratch a parting hug and then did the same with Malek, who pushed him off real quick, giving him a mere "what-up" nod. Scratch and Malek headed over to the sleeping Grady.

"Well, it was good to see ya," Ron said as he watched them walk toward Grady. Ron smiled as he looked down at the cell phone he had just lifted from Malek. He was ready to hurry off toward the hood to see what he could get for it. *Thank you, young brother.* Ron chuckled to himself, thanking Malek for providing the means to his next high.

Scratch approached Grady and saw that he was deep into a dope fiend lean, and he began to nudge him, trying to wake him. "Wake up, sonabitch." Scratch knew it was damn near impossible to take a dope fiend out of his nod, so he was going to have to take some drastic measures. He grabbed Grady by the collar and shook him.

"What this raggedy mu'fucka going to be able to tell you about Mitch?" Malek said, getting frustrated. Malek covered his mouth and nose as the strong odor of all the junkies became almost unbearable. The smell of blood from the heroin addicts and their body odor was enough to make any man vomit, but Malek tried his best to cope.

Scratch began to unbutton the man's pants. "He's going to be able to tell me anything I need to know."

"What the fuck you doing, Scratch?" Malek turned his head away.

"I am waking his ass up," Scratch said as he pulled down the man's pants, exposing his small tool. He then reached onto the ground and grabbed a handful of water from a puddle. He tilted his hand and allowed the water to pour from his hand and onto Grady's private.

"This is the only way you know how to wake a nigga up out of a nod?"

"Trust me, I know," Scratch said, trying to hurry up and get it over with. "I done had plenty of water, snow, and ice on my balls in the past waking me up out of a dope fiend lean."

Seconds later, Grady jumped when he felt the wetness on him.

"Wake up, Grady!" Scratch said as Grady was coming to.

Slowly, Grady opened his eyes. "Scratch, what's happening, playa?" he said in a slurred voice.

"What's up?" Scratch replied. "I need for you to wake up." Scratch grabbed him by the collar once again. When he saw Grady was about to nod again, he laid a powerful smack on the left side of his face, leaving a handprint on his cheek.

Grady's eyes shot open. "Damn, Scratch! Slow down!"

Scratch slapped him again, this time waking him up

completely. "I need some info about Mitch," Scratch said, getting right to the point. He knew he was messing up his man's coma-like high, but time was of the essence.

"North Side Mitch?" Grady sat up and wiped the slob drooling down his chin.

"Yeah," Malek chimed in, now that their source of information appeared to be wide-awake and alert to the questioning.

"What about him?" Grady asked.

"I know you know where his spot is at."

"His main spot," Malek added.

"We need to know where he stashes all of the dope and cash," Scratch continued, hoping Grady could tell him something.

Grady was a veteran junkie. Although Scratch had several years of being hooked on dope under his belt, Grady was up on him by a good ten years, and it showed in his appearance.

Scratch still had somewhat of a swagger, while Grady appeared worn, burned-out, and seemed to have no hope of rehabilitating himself. His hands were swollen five times their usual size from shooting so much dope into his veins. Some people on the streets call it "elephant hands," when a person's limbs swell up so bad from heroin.

Grady was a viable asset to major pushers. They would ask him to test the drug and its potency. If it was strong enough to get Grady high, it was strong enough for the public. Mitch had used Grady for that very reason on a few occasions, so Scratch knew there was a good chance

Grady would know something that might be able to help them out on hitting Mitch's spot.

Grady looked at Scratch, and for a minute, it seemed as though he was about to speak, but then his entire demeanor changed when he looked over at Malek after remembering he was standing there. Grady knew exactly who Malek was. He spat, "I don't know shit."

In the past, Grady had often approached Malek or some of his workers to ask them for a free sample, or to ask if he could get a pass on coming short. Grady would sometimes come with eight dollars instead of ten, or with change he'd scrambled up. It never failed that Malek and his other workers would deny him, embarrassing and humiliating him.

One time, after a half-hour of begging and pleading, Grady had just convinced one of Malek's workers to let him slide with being $1.50 short. The boy had stuck to his guns, refusing to let Grady slide, but Grady hung around so long agitating the boy with his presence, even begging from paying customers to make up for his shortage.

The kid finally gave in. "All right. Damn, old man!" the boy had said to Grady, sucking his teeth and rolling his eyes. "Give me what you got and then get the fuck on. You bad for business, and you smell like shit."

Grady damn near danced a jig as he collected the eight one-dollar bills and two quarters from his pocket. He handed the money over to the boy, who counted it.

Shaking his head, the boy dug a ten-dollar cop from his pocket and dangled it in the air. "I promise on everything, old man," the boy said, "you better come up with my dollar fifty. And don't think you gon' make a habit out of this shit. You ever come at me short again, I'm just gon' shoot your ass on GP. I don't care if you only twenty-five cents short next time, you ain't copping. Now take this shit and be gone."

Just as the boy was about to hand over the dope, a hand tightened around his wrist, preventing him from doing so.

"What's this about somebody being short?"

The boy turned around to see his boss, Malek, standing there. "Oh, uh, nothing," he stammered, knowing he'd been caught breaking one of the rules of slinging.

Malek said to his worker, "I know you ain't trying to lie to me. Are you, fam?"

"Uh, no, it ain't even like that. I mean, it's no big deal. Home boy here just short a dollar fifty. That's all. He's good for it." The boy looked to Grady for reassurance. "Ain't that right, old man?"

"Uh, yeah," Grady co-signed, reaching for the dope. With a carrot dangling in front of him, he would have said anything.

Malek couldn't help but chuckle. "So you got a dope fiend vouching for you now?" he asked, still gripping the boy's wrist. "And I'm supposed to be cool with that."

The boy was at a loss for words, realizing how stupid he sounded.

"All right," Malek said, finally letting his wrist loose. "If he says he's good for it, then go ahead and let him slide."

At that point, Grady was dang near salivating over the

dangling bag of dope and was glad to hear the boy granted permission to let him have it. But just as the boy went to hand Grady the dope, Malek snatched it from his hand, cold-cocking the boy with the back of his hand.

"Mu'fucka, what the fuck are the rules about letting niggas fall short?"

When the boy didn't answer Malek quickly enough, he cold-cocked him again, this time drawing blood from the boy's bottom lip. "If you let one muthufucka come up short, then every broke nigga on the block gon' come to us like we the damn Salvation Army or something, giving shit away for free." Malek continued to scold the young worker. "Nigga, this is my product. This is my reputation. You got that, fam?"

"Yeah, Malek, man," the boy said, wiping the blood from his lip. "My bad. It won't happen again."

"You damn right, it won't happen again. Get the fuck out of here!"

Without asking any questions, the young'un left the scene, leaving only Grady, Malek, and a few bystanders standing there.

"So, uh, yo, can I get that?" Grady said, pointing to the bag of dope.

Malek spat, "If you don't get the fuck outta my face . . ."

"But yo' boy got my eight dollars and fifty cents. Can I at least get eight dollars and fifty cents worth?"

Malek could feel the old man's pain, but business was business. He'd noticed a small crowd had formed, and he had a reputation to uphold on the streets. Unfortunately,

Grady would become an example. Malek sent him on his way, via a kick in the ass and a string of expletives, causing the onlookers to laugh.

As Grady stood there and thought back to the several humiliating encounters with Malek and his boys, he knew Malek didn't have a clue who he was. *Now this mu'fucka needs my help,* he thought. *I'm not giving his ass nothing. Nada. Zilch!* Not even if Malek were to offer him all the free samples in the world right now would Grady consider helping the young punk.

Scratch looked at Malek and motioned for him to give Grady something. Malek reached in his pocket and tossed a twenty-dollar bill at Grady.

No matter who a dope fiend was beefing with, the possibility of getting a high always quickly made them forgive and forget. The sight of the twenty-dollar bill washed away every thought Grady had just been thinking, and as he examined the bill as best he could for authenticity, he suddenly began to remember some vital information regarding Mitch.

Grady quickly put the twenty in his pocket and reconsidered his earlier stance. *Well, maybe just helping him out with a little bit of information won't hurt. After all, he just paid for my afternoon snack. Now I won't have to be on E.* Grady licked his ashy lips and began to sing like a bird.

"Well, I'm not for sure if it's his main stash spot or not, but I do know he has a spot off of Welch Avenue where he keeps a whole lot of dope."

Malek looked at him, his eyes silently asking Grady, *How would you know that?*

Reading Malek's unspoken words, Grady continued. "I know this because when he got a big shipment in last week, he told me to meet him over there. He didn't have time to take me to the known stash spots, so he let me taste the drug right there on the spot. It was some good shit too!" Grady thought about the potency of the drug and how good the high felt.

Grady had Malek's undivided attention. "Who does he keep at that spot?"

"I forgot." Grady glanced down at Malek's pocket then back at Malek. Just from the desperation in Malek's eyes alone, Grady could tell that the information was worth more than twenty dollars. He was sitting on the edge of his seat, like he'd been watching a whodunit for the past two hours and was only seconds away from finding out who had done it. Grady had to take advantage of Malek's vulnerable situation.

Taking note of Grady's wandering eyes, Malek grabbed another twenty and tossed it at him. "Like I asked, who does he keep at the spot?" he repeated.

With Grady's memory suddenly refreshed, he told Malek exactly what he wanted to know. "As far as I know, his sister stays there and watches over the money. It's a hush-hush spot, and nobody is supposed to know about it. He doesn't do any business out of the house. He just keeps the dope there, and she does all the counting there."

"So it's just a female up in there, huh?" Malek was surprised to hear that the only thing between him and hitting up Mitch's main stash spot was a broad. He thought he'd taught his prodigy much better than that.

"A bitch is right. A female dog, for sure." Grady nodded his head. "She is a loud, crazy bitch too! Personally, I don't care for her ass at all."

Malek looked over to Scratch as if things just might turn out good for them after all. They'd taken on big, burly security guards. Surely the two of them could handle some chick.

Grady noticed the eye contact between Malek and Scratch. "Don't get it fucked up, though. She is as feisty as they come. Worse than some dudes. What are y'all trying to do anyway?" Grady decided to be nosy, see what information he could get out of Malek and Scratch. One never knows. He might be able to take some information back to Mitch and make some more get-high money.

Knowing just how much he could trust Grady, Scratch replied, "Thanks for the information, Grady. Good lookin' out." Scratch then looked up at Malek, giving him the signal that it was time for them to split.

"A'ight then," Grady said. "But know that Mitch ain't to be tested . . . if you know what I mean."

"Take it easy, Grady," Scratch said, ignoring his friend's comment.

"You take it easy too, and whatever happens, y'all didn't get that little bit of information from me either, because I don't want any trouble with that young man. He'll whup my ass all up and down the expressway." Grady thought about what Mitch would do to him if he found out he was giving away such valuable information.

"Fuck Mitch!" Malek said. "Scratch, let's go!" Malek did a 180 and began to walk away, and Scratch followed.

Mitch's sister was about to get paid a surprise visit by Malek and Scratch, who were both prepared to walk into a situation unknown. Desperate times call for desperate measures.

Chapter Six

Keesha sat in Sweets' brand-new strip club feeling like the queen bee. Money was flowing lovely for everyone since Mitch had taken over the city. Due to this steady flow of cash, Sweets had upgraded to a new club. The old-school beef between North and South was dead.

Keesha was no longer a measly bartender. She was now a stripper and an official Manolo Mami, a title she'd been seeking for years. Her dream had come true, the same way little blonde-haired and blue-eyed girls dreamed of being Miss America.

Although Manolo was locked up, the name had stuck because of the girls' notorious reputation around Flint. The Manolo Mamis were the shit and were known for having the best head game in the city. Keesha was now the HBIC of the clique. Sweets had demoted Tasha for disloyalty and could no longer trust her, leaving room for Keesha to come up in the game and be his bottom bitch.

Keesha didn't necessarily enjoy what she had to do to stay on top. With Sweets being bisexual, he usually liked to do things in the bed that she wasn't into, but she held her tongue to keep her spot. When he put her on Mitch, Keesha happily obliged, never objecting or even voicing an opinion. She simply did as she was told, which kept her in Sweets' favor.

Keesha sat in front of the lighted vanity in the dressing room of the club as she waited for her set to begin. She looked at Tasha's reflection in her mirror and turned up her nose. She disliked everything about Tasha.

Keesha remembered the days when Tasha, Mimi, and Halleigh were official. *Those bitches had their heads in the clouds. Hating-ass hoes were always looking down on me like they were better than me or something. Now look who's laughing. The bitch came begging for her spot back, but it's taken. This shit is all me.* She rolled her eyes in the mirror as she watched Tasha open up her locker.

Keesha hated Tasha, Halleigh, and Mimi with a passion, to say the least, because when they were on top, they always reminded her that she didn't belong, making it their business to make her feel like a nobody. They gave a new definition to "mean girls." No matter how hard Keesha tried to be down, they never accepted her.

As the so-called madam of the organization, Tasha was supposed to make everybody feel accepted, but when it came to Keesha, she did no such thing. Tasha was partial to Mimi from the very beginning, and when Mimi brought Halleigh home, it was a wrap. Halleigh officially became "little sister" material to Tasha, a spot Keesha had kissed ass for, only to be overlooked.

Things had taken a change for the better, though, as far as Keesha was concerned. She was no longer on the outside looking in. Mimi was dead, and let Keesha tell it, she got what was coming to her. So there was definitely no love lost.

Now Halleigh was getting exactly what she had coming to her as well. Keesha used to play background, sitting back, watching Halleigh walk around like her shit didn't stink. It was as if Halleigh was Beyoncé. *I bet she ain't so high and mighty now.* Keesha laughed on the inside at Halleigh being held hostage by Mitch. *That's what the fuck she gets.*

When Mitch had first told Keesha about how soft Malek really was now that he had his little Barbie doll in custody, she knew Mitch was only telling her because he still felt embarrassed at the way Malek had made him look like a punk in front of her. This was Mitch's way of telling her to look at who the punk was now.

For a minute, she even doubted there was any truth to the kidnapping . . . until Mitch let her view Halleigh through the camera. Keesha almost felt sorry for the vision before her, but those feelings quickly disappeared as Keesha thought to herself, *If the bitch had treated me like I existed, I might have even tried to help her out. But fuck her!*

* * *

Keesha applied makeup to her face. She was a pretty girl, but she had a fucked-up attitude, which had gotten her fucked up plenty of times by girls from around the way. It wasn't just the Manolo Mamis who didn't really care for her, but pretty much every chick she encountered. She had a nasty disposition about her that made people not want to associate with her. Unfortunately, too busy making the rest of the world out to be the bad guy, she didn't see this flaw in herself. She always had something to say about everybody, and now that she was in not only Sweets' favor, but Mitch's favor as well, she thought she was untouchable. *All these bitches can suck a dick.*

Everybody knew her new position because she made sure of it. Her mouth was always running, and today was no different. "Hey, Tasha girl!" she said, faking friendship. She looked Tasha up and down, admiring her tall, curvaceous frame, and hating on her at the same time.

Tasha looked toward Keesha and replied with a weak, "Hey." Her words were dry. She didn't have too much kickit for Keesha. She never had. From day one, she'd always been able to read Keesha like a book and knew she wasn't to be trusted, so she dealt with her with a long-handled spoon.

"You all right?" Keesha feigned concern. She was really just doing what she always did—picking, just to see what type of beans Tasha might spill.

Keesha had learned that she may run her mouth a lot, but her words were calculated. Other people, if she gave them a chance, would just run their mouths, not even thinking about what they were saying, always giving her some type of ammunition that she could eventually use against them or somebody else.

A prime example is the time she was giving a female a private lap dance in the back room. The girl was straight, as in not gay, and she and her friends had just decided to come to a strip club for the fun of it. Then when her friends dared her to get a lap dance, chipping in to pay for it themselves, after a few shots, the girl gave in.

In the back room, Keesha had no problem dancing on the girl for the two songs her friends had paid for at twenty-five dollars each. The girl giggled and laughed all the way through the first song, as Keesha rubbed on her and grinded on her. Keesha knew the girl wouldn't have been down for it if she wasn't liquored. It also wasn't hard for her to detect that the giggling was a nervous reaction. In order to take the girl's mind off things, Keesha engaged in conversation while she danced the second song.

The song wasn't even halfway over before Keesha learned that ol' girl was the bottom bitch of a young baller coming up in the game in Detroit. She ran her mouth so much about dude, Keesha got enough information on him to set him up to be robbed. So, on top of the fifty dollars she'd earned for obtaining the information, she got five Gs from the proceeds of the robbery. Knowing just how much getting a chick to run her mouth could benefit her, Keesha tried to play nice with Tasha.

But Tasha knew better and could see right through Keesha's fake-friend role. *Bitch, please,* Tasha said to herself in her head. *Your mu'fuckin' ass is as transparent as Saran Wrap. What the fuck you want?*

Tasha continued to dress for her set, not even giving Keesha the courtesy of pretending they were friends. "Can I help you with something, Keesha?" she asked as she put on her M.A.C. cosmetics.

Although Tasha could barely afford the high-priced makeup now that she had fallen off, she still refused to wear anything less. A part of her felt shame for going back to the life of a stripper. Sweets pretty much owned her and had a price tag on her ass, and whoever had the most money could get it; but she wanted so much more in life. She felt like she was selling her soul to the devil all over again. She had been here and done all this before. Now her life had come full circle and she was back to square one.

"I was just trying to check on you, girl," Keesha said. "I know you've been kind of distant ever since you came back. I know it's probably awkward with me being the head girl in this piece, but I want you to know you can talk to me, girl. We're peoples. So if you ever need to talk to someone, just know you can always come holler at me," Keesha said, piling on the sweetness.

Tasha scoffed and shook her head. "Yeah, a'ight. We're people." Tasha knew Keesha was trying to remind her that she'd taken her spot, but Keesha didn't realize the joke was on her. *There ain't no fucking way in the world I would be fucking Sweets' gay ass. Shit, at least Manolo was fine. Sweets' ass is ugly as fuck, and the nigga is a booty bandit. Dumb bitch probably don't even make the nigga strap up.*

Keesha heard the sarcasm in Tasha's voice. She lowered her eyes in a disgusted gaze. "Take it however you want. I'm just letting you know I'm here. From the looks of things, you can use all the friends you can get. Ain't none of these new bitches trying to fuck with you, because you snaked Manolo, and that reputation makes them not trust you. But I've been around for a minute. I know the deal. You're a real bitch, and us real bitches got to stick together."

"Um," Tasha simply said as she sat down and oiled her toned legs. *I wish this bitch would keep it moving. If she thinks I'm about to fall for her fake-ass bullshit lines, she's got another think coming.*

"I know after your brother died you've been less talkative. That's fucked up how Halleigh was all up in your face, and now she's laid up with the nigga that killed your peoples," Keesha said, adding insult to injury.

Tasha cringed at the mention of Maury. She wanted to smack the shit out of Keesha for bringing it up. Tasha had gone many sleepless nights thinking of her loss and Halleigh's betrayal. Tasha felt like Halleigh was fake for choosing Malek over their friendship. She would have never chosen a dude over one of her girls. Being in the business she was in, she knew dudes were all the same, and at the end of the day, they'd choose money over bitches any day. So why should a bitch choose them over anything else?

When Maury was alive, he had strong feelings for Halleigh, and Halleigh was game, until fate brought Malek back into her life. When Maury turned up dead at the hands of Malek and Halleigh still chose to be with him, Tasha was through with Halleigh. After all she had done for her, she couldn't believe the choice Halleigh made. With Keesha bringing all that back to her remembrance, she was hurting inside, but not tipping her hand to Keesha, who was still standing in her face.

"I'm good on that conversation, Keesha," Tasha said. "You didn't even know my brother, so it'd be best if you wouldn't speak on that . . . ever." Tasha hoped that Keesha took the words as a threat, because she certainly meant for them to be.

"I hear you," Keesha said, putting her hands up in surrender. "My fault, Tasha. I know that's a sensitive subject, but just so you know, that bitch Halleigh is gonna get hers. Matter of fact, she's getting hers now."

Before Keesha knew it, the tables had been turned without much effort on Tasha's part, and Keesha began to run her mouth, all in the name of trying to lure Tasha to run hers.

Tasha wondered what Keesha meant by, "She's getting hers now." It didn't take her too long to figure it out, as Keesha filled her in on the details of Halleigh's whereabouts.

"Mitch got that bitch tied up in the basement as we speak." Keesha leaned in so that the two other chicks who'd just entered the room wouldn't overhear her. "I don't know what it is about this ho, but she had that nigga all googly-eyed too. I put the work in, though, and switched that nigga's train of thought real quick—Malek is the enemy, and so is his bitch. She won't be breathing long."

Keesha rambled on, thinking it was safe to speak on the situation to Tasha. After the way Halleigh had played both Tasha and her now dead brother, Keesha assumed Tasha would just as well want Halleigh to die in that basement after her disloyalty. Little did Keesha know, she couldn't have been more wrong.

Although Tasha felt played by Halleigh, the two had been through far too much together for her to just flat out wish her dead. She and Halleigh had been like sisters, and a deep-rooted bond still linked the two of them in some crazy sort of way.

Tasha's heartbeat began to speed up as Keesha spoke, but she kept her poker face on. "Damn, that's fucked up," she said with nonchalance. "I guess karma is a bitch."

"Yes, it is. I pick up money from that spot for Mitch every day and laugh every time I see her dumb ass on them cameras."

Tasha gave Keesha a slight smile and then cut her short. "All right, girl, let me get out here and make some of this money. You know how Sweets is if we come up short."

"All right then, girl. But remember what I said—if you ever need to talk, I'm here."

Now Tasha was the one painting on the fake smile, making Keesha think she'd gotten one step closer to her world. "Thanks, girl. I really appreciate it."

Tasha thought of Halleigh tied up and hurt somewhere as she exited the dressing room. A part of her wanted to smile inside and just say, "Fuck it! That's what she gets. What goes around comes around."

But the part of her that had connected with Halleigh from years of friendship wouldn't allow her to do so. Tasha couldn't help but feel guilt, knowing Halleigh was caught up in a dangerous situation. Tasha had always been protective of Halleigh, and felt as though she should do something to help her.

Chapter Seven

As Tasha received her introduction and stepped onto the stage, the thunderous applause put her mind back on her money and off Halleigh's predicament. Besides, she was no longer Halleigh's keeper, so why should she care what happened to her?

A Plies joint cranked from the DJ booth, and Tasha began to wind her body slowly. She slowly removed the fishnet cover-up she had over her skimpy two-piece neon-green thong set. With every slow wind, the two-piece appeared to be dancing in mid-air under the lights. It looked like a magic show as men became mesmerized and enthralled and money flew onto the stage.

Tasha was tempted to work the pole. She hadn't danced since she was twenty years old and didn't want to risk looking crazy, but that didn't keep her from working it out. She knew sliding down the pole would land her even more money. Dudes loved it when females did tricks on the pole. Now twenty-six, her body was just as flawless as it had been from the beginning.

Even with all the dollars flying on stage, and all the whooping and hollering going on around her by the men enjoying her set, Tasha's mind still somehow managed to drift back to Halleigh. She tried closing her eyes and continued to move her body sensually, focusing on the music that the DJ was spinning. That worked for a minute, but Halleigh's face kept popping up in her head.

She tried desperately to shake the thoughts, but she just couldn't. She could no longer hear the lyrics to the music playing, but instead heard these words dancing around in her head: *Didn't Halleigh fuck Mitch back in the day? Will he really hurt her?* Tasha was trying to convince herself that Halleigh wasn't her business. She didn't even know why she cared after the snake shit Halleigh pulled, but she had to admit, she was worried.

After hearing stories of how Mitch got down in the streets, she knew Halleigh was in danger. Mitch could be outright ruthless when it came down to it. Tasha didn't even know if there was anything she could do without getting caught up and even landing her a spot in that basement right next to Halleigh.

Tasha continued to try to convince herself not to interfere with whatever Mitch had going on. She kept going back and forth. *Why should I put my ass on the line for her? She's a fake bitch, and I'm tired of playing captain save-a-fuckin'-ho. Where has she been since Maury died? When I needed her, she was ghost with Malek. Nobody matters to her but him, so let his ass save her.*

Just the thought of Malek all of a sudden had Tasha wondering where Malek was at, and why he'd allow Mitch to pull off something like this. *Where's her knight in shining armor when she really needs his ass?*

Tasha was so busy thinking about Halleigh and Malek, she didn't even hear her song stop. Only after the second time the DJ called out to her, finally getting her attention, did she realize her set was over.

Keesha stood at the side of the stage, tapping her foot with an attitude, waiting for her to get off the stage so she could make her paper. "So you leaving all that for me?" Keesha asked sarcastically, motioning her head to the money Tasha was leaving on the stage that the men in the club had thrown her way.

"Oh, yeah, the money," Tasha said, somewhat in a daze as she went and scooped it all up.

"I should have let her ass keep it moving," Keesha said under her breath, not knowing why she'd brought it to Tasha's attention. Keesha knew sooner or later it would have dawned on Tasha, and she would have hated to have to kick her ass over a few dollars.

When Tasha had finally scooped up all of her money and made her way off stage, she went back to the dressing room to change into another outfit. She still had to work the crowd, and most importantly, the VIP. She wanted to be fresh. A stinking bitch is a broke bitch in the strip club, so she carried feminine wipes and body spray to make sure she was always on point. *He's going to kill her,* she thought as she quickly changed, still thinking about Halleigh. She leaned her head against her locker and inhaled deeply. Tasha's pride didn't want her to intervene, but her heart was all in. She tried hard to side with her mind, but her heart prevailed.

"Fuck it!" Tasha said out loud to herself. "That bitch is fake, but that's the difference between me and her. I'm a real bitch, and real bitches do real things." Tasha kept up the conversation with herself while she freshened up. "If I didn't know, then it wouldn't be my fault, but I have to help her now. I can't just do nothing. Now I just have to figure out how I'm going to get her away from Mitch."

At that moment, Keesha walked into the dressing room, her skin glossed with sweat. It was obvious she had just come off stage. "The ballers are up in this piece tonight," she exclaimed. She started counting out a mound of money.

Tasha didn't reply. Her mind was on figuring out a way to get to Halleigh.

"You a'ight?" Keesha asked Tasha. "Your mind seems to be in a whole 'nother world. It must be, for you to walk off the stage and leave all your loot."

"Yeah, girl, I'm good," Tasha replied in the nicest voice she could muster up.

As real as she liked to believe she was, she knew she had to play the role of fake friend with Keesha. Keesha was her only hope, the only link to finding out exactly where Halleigh was being held hostage, and how to get to her.

"You know what?" Tasha said in a perky voice. "It has

been a rough day, but I need to get my mind right and go make this money. Hurry up and change, so we can work these niggas in VIP."

Tasha was no longer in bitch mode. She was in pimp mode. Working underneath Manolo for all of those years, she had learned a thing or two. Keesha had met her match. Tasha, about to pimp the information she needed out of Keesha like a pro, all of a sudden was best girl-friends with Keesha.

"Girl, you ain't said nothing but a word," Keesha said. "Let's go!" Keesha knew that Tasha would eventually come around and learn to accept that she was now top dog. Like the saying goes, if you can't beat 'em, join 'em. She was glad that Tasha realized the real and decided to climb on board, and had no problem with her sudden change in attitude.

The two women exited the locker room, and Tasha led the way to VIP, dudes grabbing at her left and right along the way, trying to buy her a drink. Ordinarily, Tasha might have stopped and let a dude buy her a drink or two, considering she made even more money off the drinks. Whenever the dudes bought the girls a drink, the cost of the drink was split with the bar 60/40 in the dancer's favor. And the drinks for the dancers started at a ten-dollar minimum.

Tasha was headed straight to where the ballers played. They would go deep, with their drink minimum starting at one hundred dollars. With VIP full, she wasn't looking for a nigga with shallow pockets, and not for her own sake this time, but surprisingly, for Halleigh.

Tasha needed someone that could bait Keesha without hesitation. Money definitely couldn't be an object for that someone, which was sure to grab Keesha hook, line, and sinker. She knew Keesha needed to do the pickup for Mitch and Sweets, but if everything went as planned, Keesha would hand the job off to her and try to make a couple dollars out of one of the club's patrons.

Tasha knew that she had to attract the guy because Keesha wasn't "snag-a-hustler" material. Her body was nice, but came a dime a dozen in the hood. Her face was cute, but her nose was big as hell. She definitely wasn't model material. She was what one would call average. Nothing about her was extraordinary. Most girls with average faces made up for it with humongous assets like big butts, or nice breasts, but Keesha was lacking in both departments.

But Tasha had to give the girl credit. She got her share of dudes. Tasha knew Keesha's appeal had a lot to do with the rumors that she would do it anytime, anyplace, anyhow—for the right price, of course. She had the same tag line as Burger King; the dudes could have it their way with her.

Upon arriving in VIP, Tasha quickly spotted her "vic" in the crowd. Actually, he spotted her, grabbing her by the waist as she walked by, catching his finger in her thong.

Tasha slapped his hands away playfully. "You've got to pay to play this game, baby, but it's the best ride you'll ever get. Worth every cent," Tasha said, Keesha right beside her.

* * *

Tasha didn't have to worry about Keesha jacking her game, because there wasn't a bitch alive that could game a nigga like she could. Her swag came from years of practice. She had been got by many a nigga before she flipped the roles and started getting them. When she first got in the game, dudes used to basically throw at her whatever they felt like, because they could tell she was fresh meat. But that didn't last long. She quickly wised up, and started taking dudes for everything they and their wives had. It was her suaveness, loyalty, and dedication that convinced Manolo that she should be top dog, pulling her from working the streets to being in charge of the other girls.

But that was back then and this was now. Even so, Tasha was seasoned through and through, a thorough broad who didn't have to try too hard to get what she wanted. Her sex appeal was natural; she never had to force anyone's hand. Niggas flocked to her like flies flocked to shit, and it was all because of her confidence.

Tasha could be standing next to Buffie the Body, Melyssa Ford, or any other industry chick, and intimidation would still be foreign to her. If she wasn't the baddest bitch in the room when she entered, by the time she exited, everyone would know her name. It was all about her aura, the way she carried herself, and her confidence level—the make-up of a true diva.

She was always on top, and another chick could never outshine her. Tasha was wifey material on the outside. God had blessed her when he had molded her. But nobody was perfect, and she had her flaws about her.

Flint was small, and her promiscuous past had tainted her. Even though Tasha may have appeared to be wifey material on the outside, no man wanted to turn a ho into a housewife. As notorious as a Manolo Mami might have been, in good old-fashioned street terms, she was still considered a ho. So instead of being wifey, she was always the side chick that niggas came to when they needed some relief from the nagging ways of their main squeeze.

Tasha resented the choices she'd made in her life. She wished she could have turned back the hands of time to the beginning of her adolescence, the time when her life got crazy and she'd slipped into the clutches of Manolo. She couldn't blame it all on Manolo, though. Even though he was her pimp, he had her head because she allowed him to have it. She had always been a strong, independent woman. That's why anybody who knew Tasha back in her high school days couldn't believe she was doing the things she was known for doing today.

Back in high school, Tasha ran with the popular clique, a group of chicks that was not only beautiful, but brilliant, and stayed on the honor roll. Her teachers never had a single problem with her. Co-captain of the drill team, she'd earned varsity letters for drill team competitions. She knew she was all that, and never needed anyone to tell her, especially a man, which was why she, herself, couldn't believe she was in the predicament she was in today, turning tricks for the VIP in a strip club.

* * *

"Yo, ma, money ain't a thing," the dude in VIP told Tasha. "I got it to spend, if it's worth it. I'm trying to see you tonight after everything settle down," he said, looking her up and down and licking his lips. "What's your name?"

Same line, different nigga. Tasha tried her best not to seem bored with his lame ass. "Tasha," she replied as she leaned in to whisper in his ear in her attempt to be heard over the music. "And this is my girl, Keesha." Tasha motioned her head to Keesha, who smiled and winked her eye in what she thought was a sexy gesture. *Lame-ass bitch deserves this lame-ass nigga,* Tasha thought. *Leave the winks to the movie stars.*

"You and your girl trying to grab a room or something after this?" he asked.

"I don't even know your name, and you already asking to slide out after the club lets out?" Tasha answered with an infectious smile as Keesha played the back. "Can I at least get a name? And don't give me no nicknames. I want what's printed on your driver's license."

The handsome, thuggish guy in front of her replied, "Lamont."

"Nice to meet you, hon," Tasha said as she extended her hand.

Lamont had to laugh to himself as he accepted Tasha's hand inside of his and shook it. He usually didn't have no kick-it for strippers. They were there to do a job and help him to relax, but he found himself enjoying this back-and-forth banter with Tasha, who could see it in his eyes, too, that she already had him lured.

"Nice to meet you too, Ms. Tasha," Lamont replied. "You and your girl want a drink or something? Have a seat and chop it up with me and my niggas." He nodded toward his boys he was up in there with.

Tasha and Keesha shot them some smiles and head nods.

Lamont then went into his pocket and pulled out a wad of cash. He peeled off four hundred-dollar bills from his large money knot and handed two to each lady then motioned for them to sit down. Tasha sat down after stuffing the cash into her neon top, and Keesha followed suit, dollar signs flashing in her eyes.

For the next few minutes, although Tasha smiled at the gentlemen, danced seductively, and entertained effortlessly, her mind was still set on getting to Halleigh.

Tasha was still sipping on her same Sex on the Beach she'd had Lamont order for her, while Keesha was throwing back Long Islands like it was water. Tasha knew Keesha's intoxication would lead to loose lips, and would make it easier to get Halleigh's location out of her.

Keesha was overly sexual, if there was ever such a thing in a strip club, and was throwing it all in the ring to earn her keep, bouncing back and forth from one lap to another. Lamont and his friends seemed to be enjoying her show, too, because they were showering Keesha with different denominations of bills.

As the night came to a close, Lamont and his friends prepared to leave. "What's up, shorty? You and your friend rolling with us?" he asked.

"I'm down," Keesha answered quickly. "I just need to make

a run real quick, though. I can meet y'all at the hotel in like an hour."

"Cool." Lamont looked Tasha's way. "What about you, Ms. Tasha? You with it or what?"

Tasha shook her head. "Nah, I'ma take a rain check. My head is bangin' right now."

Lamont sucked his teeth. "What? Off of that one little drink you babysat all night? I know your tolerance is higher than that, working in this place where your real money is in the drinks."

"Baby, I'd had my share of drinks earlier," Tasha lied, rubbing her forehead for effect. "I usually can hang better than this, but I don't know what the fuck is wrong with me tonight. I'm going to have to pass, though. Come check for me next weekend. You know where I'm at." Tasha looked to Keesha. "And, Keesha, you can go ahead and roll with them now if you want. I'll handle your business here at the club for you, make your run, or whatever it was you needed to do." Tasha was extra friendly, as if she and Keesha were BFF's (best friends forever), when, in actuality, if the bitch was on fire, Tasha wouldn't waste her spit to put her out.

Keesha was all game and excited to go make that paper, but she knew she had to take care of her business. "Good looking out, Tasha, but I don't know. I got to do that thing for Mitch too," she stated, hesitation in her tone.

Lamont, obviously irritated by the fact that Tasha wasn't joining them and Keesha was acting like she wasn't down with it either, said, "Look, you trying to make this paper or not? I don't got all day."

Tasha could see the wheels in Keesha's mind churning as she decided between the possibility of making all that extra money, or making the delivery. She couldn't help but smile. Her plan was coming to fruition perfectly. But just in case, she added that little extra push. "Girl, go ahead. Just tell me where I got to go, and I'll pick that up for you and take it to your boy."

After a few more seconds of consideration and that final bit of persuasion from Tasha, Keesha decided to take Tasha up on her offer and roll with Lamont. "Okay, girl, thanks. I'm not trying to miss out on this money these niggas about to throw my way." Keesha leaned in and gave Tasha two diva kisses, one on each cheek.

Here go this bitch with this ol' made-for-TV bullshit. Tasha returned the fake love with a smile. "Just text me the address to the spot, and I'll handle it," Tasha assured her. "Have fun, and call me when you get in to let me know you're safe." Tasha then pointed a finger at Lamont. "Take care of my girl."

Lamont nodded and winked at Tasha, then he and his boys slid out of the club with Keesha in the midst of them.

Chapter Eight

As soon as Tasha saw Keesha leave out of the club, she hightailed it back to the dressing room. "I've got to get to Halleigh," she whispered to herself as she threw on a pair of skintight jeans and a Deréon hoodie.

She hurriedly slipped her feet into a pair of black peep-toes and stalked out of the club. Security at the club usually walked the girls out, but Tasha was in too much of a hurry to wait on an escort. After making it safely to her car, she threw her Nike gym bag in her trunk and then got into her car. She pulled out her cell phone and checked her messages. No new text or voice messages. "Come on, Keesha, send me the address," she said impatiently as she sat in the car.

After waiting another five minutes, she finally got the text. "Bing!" she said with a smile. She put her car in drive and burnt rubber out of the parking lot as she headed to the north side of Flint.

As Tasha drove through Selby hood, goose bumps formed on her arms, and the hair on the back of her neck stood up. The hood was too quiet, which wasn't normal at all. It was the middle of the summer, and no one was out. Even the streetlights were blown out, and the banging of dudes flossing their subwoofers was non-existent. But the hood wasn't the only thing on Tasha's mind right now. She couldn't help but wonder how many of Mitch's goons were guarding Halleigh.

Why am I even putting myself out here for this girl? For a minute she wanted to turn the car around and hit the I-75, headed back to the South Side, where she was most comfortable, but she didn't.

After a few minutes, she located the house address that Keesha had texted her, and put her game face on. Although her insides were twisted in knots and her guts were like liquid fire, on the outside she was cool, calm, and collected. After taking a deep breath, Tasha got out of the car and headed toward the house, her heels clicking on the pavement as she made her way up the driveway.

In the text, Keesha had instructed her to use the back door, so that's exactly where she went. After opening the screen on the back door, she knocked and waited patiently for someone to answer. At first, no one came to the door, so she knocked again. When once again there was no answer, she reached for her phone to double-check the address on the text Keesha had sent her, to make sure that she was in fact at the correct house.

Before she could even pull her phone out, the door swung open, and a dark-skinned guy with a fresh Caesar looked her up and down. "What's good?" He looked over Tasha's shoulder as if he was expecting someone else to be with her. He then looked back to her and said, "You definitely ain't Keesha, ma. Who you here to see?"

"Yeah, Keesha got caught up, so Mitch sent me over here to take care of the pickup." Tasha watched the guy ogle her as he puffed the blunt between his dark fingers. "What the fuck, nigga? Is you gon' let me in or what? You staring, like that's gon' get you any closer to this pussy. Come off them dollars, and we might be able to talk about something. Other than that, let's keep it moving and handle this business."

Tasha made her way into the house and moved past dude, but just as she suspected, his eyes were glued to her behind. "Where everybody at?" she asked casually after scoping out the place.

"Whose everybody, baby girl?" Dude closed the door and locked it. "It's just me and you, so let's take advantage of this opportunity." He moved up on Tasha and put his hands around her waist, a sinister smile on his face.

At first, Tasha was thinking about kneeing him right in his nuts, but then she caught a glimpse of the monitor that displayed Halleigh on the screen. Now she had a sinister smile on her face, as her plan was working out better and quicker than she expected.

There was only one thing, though. She didn't expect to see Halleigh chilling in a bed. Tasha could have sworn Keesha had told her that Mitch was holding Halleigh in a basement. *Exaggerating-ass bitch,* Tasha thought. She could have kicked herself for believing Keesha's story. For all she knew, Keesha could have been setting her up.

As Tasha observed the monitor more closely, even though Halleigh wasn't being kept in a basement, it still looked as though she was being kept against her will. From what Tasha could see, Halleigh was crying or had been crying. Her eyes looked puffy, and her hair looked as though it hadn't seen a hairdresser in days. She lay in the bed almost in a fetal position. Back in the day, Tasha might have even figured Halleigh was up in there making some money, but she knew better, since Halleigh had left the game alone when she cut up her Manolo Mami card.

The dude's hands seemed to be slipping lower down Tasha's waist and onto her butt. Most dudes knew not to touch the merchandise without making a down payment. *Fuck it, Tasha! Do what you have to do to get your girl and bounce,* Tasha thought. She then began to grind her behind into his crotch seductively.

"Don't play," he said as he continued to get blunted.

Tasha took the blunt from his lips. "*You* don't play." She hit the hydro. "You got the money?"

"Oh, it's like that? You don't want to play a little bit? You know what they say about all work and no play."

"I know what they say about all play with no pay." Tasha winked.

"I feel you, ma. I got you." He once again looked Tasha up and down, releasing her from his clutch. "But I can see you are the type of chick that likes to handle her business first."

On that note, the guy opened a kitchen cabinet and pulled out a medium-sized canvas bag full of money rolls. He handed the bag to Tasha.

Tasha inconspicuously looked at Halleigh through the monitors but didn't speak on it. She simply acted like she belonged. The dude was so distracted by her presence, he couldn't take his eyes off her and didn't even confirm that Mitch had actually sent her.

"You see something you like?" Tasha flirted.

The guy nodded lazily as he tucked his bottom lip into his mouth. He approached Tasha and didn't hesitate before covering her lips with his own. His hands roamed all over her body.

Tasha didn't usually kiss niggas in the mouth, but she went for broke. He tasted like weed, and Tasha was hoping that his being high would work to her advantage.

Tasha began to reciprocate, moving her hands along his body. She made a mental note of the gun she felt on his waistline. His hands moved with experience as he undid the button on the top of her jeans.

She allowed his hands to touch her body because she needed him to trust her. She pulled his shirt over his head and then removed his pistol. She allowed him to strip her down to her bra and panties, while she removed all of his clothing. He stood before her naked as the day he was born, confident with what he was packing. She understood why, because he was blessed in every physical way.

She caressed his manhood and licked on his neck then whispered, "Sit down, daddy. I want to ride you."

Unable to conceal his excitement, he sat down in the dining room chair.

Tasha backed away slowly, as if she was about to dance for him. "I want to dance for you, daddy. Close your eyes," she instructed.

The potential to hit a chick as tight as Tasha made the dude lose his mind. He obediently did as he was told, which was a big mistake on his part.

Tasha grabbed his gun, and in one quick motion, knocked him out with the steel. She swung twice, both times hitting him as hard as she possibly could. He fell to the floor, blood on his temple, and he wasn't moving.

Tasha moved into action. Her heart was beating out of her chest. She didn't want to yell because she was afraid to awaken the guy on the floor. Although she knew that she should shoot him, she couldn't. She wasn't a killer. So, she prayed that he'd stay out cold long enough for her to do what she had to do.

Tasha quickly began opening up doors and looking in rooms. When none appeared to be the room she'd observed Halleigh in, she immediately ran up the stairs to the second floor. "Halleigh!" she called out quietly as she made her way around the second floor, constantly looking over her shoulder.

Halleigh thought she was dreaming when she heard a female voice call her name, so she didn't reply. But then she heard it again and shot straight up in the bed. She recognized that voice.

"Halleigh!" Tasha called out again.

"Tasha?" she answered, her voice scratchy from not talking. "Tasha, is that you? Please, I'm in here," she yelled. She went to the door and tried to open it, but it was locked from the outside. "Tasha!" Halleigh frantically began to try the doorknob.

Tasha tried to open the door from her side as well, to no avail. "Damn it! Hold on, Halleigh! I've got to go get the key!"

"Tasha, no! Don't leave me here!" Halleigh screamed.

"Halleigh, I'm coming back. I can't open this door without the key. Just sit tight."

Tasha crept back down the stairs with the gun aimed, ready to fire. Her arm was like spaghetti, and her hand shook violently. She had to take a minute to breathe in order to calm down before she walked back onto the first floor. As soon as she rounded the corner, she was bum-rushed onto the floor.

"Bitch! I'ma kill your ass!" The guy smacked the taste from Tasha's mouth, causing the gun to slide across the floor.

Tasha frantically crawled to reach it, but the guy pulled her legs so hard, her face hit the floor, and she instantly felt her nose burst and tasted blood in her mouth. "Aghh!" she screamed as she swung her fists with power and connected with his chin.

This only infuriated her assailant more. He started throwing blows her way, and she saw lights every time he cracked her head. Tasha couldn't overpower him. He was too strong, and if she kept fighting back, both her and Halleigh would more than likely end up six feet under. "Okay, stop! Please stop!" Tasha pleaded.

"Bitch on that grimy shit," the guy said to himself. He pried Tasha's legs open. "You should've just gave me this shit. Now I'ma take it." He began to unbuckle his belt and unbutton his pants.

Tasha's eyes glazed over as she was taken back to the first time she had been raped. She'd never imagined in her worst nightmare that it would be happen to her all over again.

She slammed her eyes shut tightly as her attacker violated her. She told herself that she couldn't allow this to happen to her again. So, with the last little bit of strength she could muster up, she instinctively brought her knee up and hit him in the balls as hard as she could.

"Ohh, shit!!!" he screamed in pain as he grabbed himself and rolled off her. "Fucking bitch!" he said, panting wildly.

Tasha's eyes darted around the room until she spotted the gun. She scrambled toward the gun, crawling like a snake. She was only a good three inches from the gun when her attacker quickly rebounded, once again pulling at her legs.

"Noooo!" Tasha began to scream out in fear as she kicked as hard as she could, hoping she was doing some kind of damage to the guy. She could feel her body being pulled farther and farther away from the gun. "God, please help me!" She snatched one of her ankles from his grip and turned from her stomach to her side so that her other leg twisted in his grip. With a clear shot of the perpetrator, Tasha pulled her leg up and then flushed it down into his face with all her might.

The powerful blow loosened his grip from her ankle, allowing her one more chance at freedom. Managing to get up on all fours, Tasha crawled over to the gun. As soon as her hand reached the steel, she could once again feel his hands wrap around her legs. Without even thinking twice about it, Tasha brought the gun up, closed her eyes, and then pulled the trigger several times. She didn't realize it was over until she heard his body hit the floor in a loud thump. When she opened her eyes, he was lying right beside her, his eyes wide open and staring into hers.

The crimson red blood poured from a hole in the side of his neck, and he twitched while his eyes pleaded for Tasha to help him. There was nothing she could do for him now. Not that she would, even if she could. He was the enemy, and there was no telling what he would have done to her if she hadn't shot him. Still, Tasha couldn't believe the man next to her would die by her hands.

She avoided looking him in his dying eyes and began to pat his body down until she retrieved the key that would set Halleigh free. After going through both front pockets and coming up short, she finally found one single key in his left back pocket. That had to be the key she was looking for.

Gripping the key in the palm of her hand, Tasha ran up the stairs full speed and put the key in the lock. Her hands were shaking so badly, she could barely unlock the door.

"Tasha, is that you?" Halleigh asked from the other side of the door. She'd heard commotion and screams coming from downstairs as she had waited with her ear to the door for Tasha to return. She prayed the entire time that whatever was going on down those stairs, Tasha would come out on top.

Right when Halleigh spoke, Tasha finally managed to unlock the door.

As it opened, Halleigh backed away, hoping her prayer was answered and that Tasha would walk through that door. When Tasha entered the room, Halleigh was standing in the middle of the room, worry and fear written on her face.

"Oh, Hal," Tasha said as she and Halleigh ran toward each other. They hugged like the long-lost sisters they were. Any animosity Tasha once held for Halleigh was out of the window. "Are you okay?"

Halleigh, flooded with relief when she saw Tasha's face, was too emotional to respond, but she nodded her head.

"We have to get out of here," Tasha said. She knew there was a possibility someone could come to the house at any moment, and she didn't want to be there if they did. She didn't want to have to kill again. She would if she had to, but if she could avoid doing so, that would be better.

She quickly wrapped her arms around Halleigh and guided her down the steps and toward the door. "Wait," she said, stopping in her tracks before they exited the house.

"Tasha? Come on, let's get out of here," Halleigh pleaded.

Tasha went and grabbed the bag of money and took the gun she'd used to kill the dude. After taking one last look at the body, she ran to the back door, helped Halleigh to the car, and then got ghost into the night.

"Tasha, I have to find Malek. He's going to kill him," Halleigh said as she rode in the passenger's seat.

Tasha shook her head in disgust. She couldn't believe the only thing on Halleigh's mind right now was that nigga Malek. She was the one who had come to her rescue, not Malek. If he was all that, how did she end up being held hostage in the first place? There had to come a time when Halleigh got over her addiction to Malek, and how Tasha saw it, the time was now.

"Halleigh, tell me one thing. You know Malek killed Maury—I know you're not stupid. I've been here for you since I've known you, and you said fuck me, to be with this nigga. When you were trapped up with Manolo, Malek never came for you. He was doing it up with Jamaica Joe while you were being pimped all over the city. You were just kidnapped behind this nigga's bullshit, I'm sure, and when I come save your ass, once again, the first thing you say is not 'thank you, Tasha,' but you on some 'save Malek' bullshit. Why?"

"Because I love him. I've always loved him. You know that, Tasha," Halleigh explained. "I know you don't understand. I don't expect you to." Halleigh stared out of the window. "But it's always about him, from the beginning, and you know that. Nothing has changed. No matter what Malek and I go through, that will never change. My life without him equals death."

Halleigh's answer floored Tasha. She had never felt

love like that before, but it was at that moment she realized Halleigh, following the same script from the very beginning, hadn't changed up on her.

Halleigh had always been about Malek. From the very first day Tasha had met her, she was addicted to him like crack. If things ever came down to Halleigh having to choose, Malek would win every time, and Tasha knew that.

Unfortunately, Tasha had opened her heart and found a dear friend in Halleigh, only to be disappointed because Halleigh's loyalty lay with Malek first and foremost. Tasha felt it was impossible for her to ever love another person on the level that Halleigh loved Malek, but it wasn't her place to judge. The only thing Tasha had was her word, which she'd kept by getting Halleigh out.

"Just get some rest, Hal. We're going to go back to my crib, so I can grab some clothes and personal things. Mitch is going to come looking for me because Keesha will tell him she sent me to the house. It's not going to take him long to put two and two together. So it looks like I'm going to be on the run again." A sad disposition took over Tasha's tone. "I just wish I had Maury to run to this time."

Halleigh looked over at Tasha and rested her hand on top of hers.

"I love you, Hal, but I can't forget or forgive what Malek did to my brother," Tasha told her. "I love you, not him. I'll help you get yourself together, but after that, you're on your own. I'm getting out of town as soon as possible."

Chapter Nine

"**A**ghh!" Keesha screamed as Mitch slapped her with brute force, sending her head jerking to the side.

"Bitch, what the fuck were you thinking? You don't change my play. You just play your fucking position." Mitch paced back and forth in a rage. "You told this bitch where my stash spot was? Are you out of your fucking mind? Now one of my niggas is in the dirt, I'm out of a hundred grand, and Halleigh escaped!"

Keesha could see the hint of red flecks of rage behind Mitch's eyes. She cringed as he raised his hand to her once more, knowing that this ass-whupping was not going to be a short one. "Please, Mitch," she said, attempting to block one of his blows.

"Please, Mitch, my ass!" he barked as he continued his pacing.

Keesha wiped the back of her hand across her lip and

looked down at the blood from her busted lip. "I'm sorry. I didn't know. I was just trying to make us some money, baby. I was doing this for you," she lied, thinking quick on her feet. She had no intention of giving Mitch a cut from any of the money she'd made with Lamont and his boys. She screamed, "I had no idea she was going for Halleigh!"

"It doesn't matter if you knew or not! Bitch, use deductive reasoning. It's fucking common sense!" Mitch put his hands around her small neck and squeezed tightly.

Her eyes bulged as she felt Mitch threatening to end her life. He wasn't choking her, but the threat of death was fresh. He pushed her against the wall and lifted her feet off the ground a bit, applying more pressure to her fragile neck. She instinctively brought her hands up in an attempt to get out of his hold.

"Bitch, you gon' work all my fucking paper off. You no longer come and go as you like. You belong to me until further notice. Halleigh may have gotten away, but, bitch, now you gon' take her place." Mitch let Keesha go, and she fell to her knees.

"Okay, daddy, I'll work it off for you right now," she whispered desperately as she grasped at his belt buckle. She would do anything to keep her spot. If she could just put her head game on him, then his anger would lessen, but the familiar language of "bitch slap" brought her back to reality.

"Bitch, get your hands off of me and get your worthless ass out there and make my fucking money. I don't give a damn if you got to get it penny by penny. You bring it all back here. And if I have to come looking for you, then that's your ass. I won't be doing all this talking next time. I'ma dead your ass." Mitch dragged her out of the house and slammed the door in her face.

"Fuck!" he screamed, knocking a lamp off his end table. He collapsed on his couch and put his head in his hands. He couldn't help but laugh to himself. Halleigh had slipped out of his clutches, and now his hold on Malek was non-existent. Both his money and Halleigh were gone. Mitch wouldn't have even been as pissed if Tasha had simply just gotten him for the bag of money. With the ransom he would have made off Malek, he wouldn't have even missed that, but now he no longer had a "marker."

Mitch pulled the .45 pistol from his waist and set it next to him. He had to be careful. Even with Halleigh gone and probably back in Malek's arms, Malek wasn't going to let this shit ride. He knew he'd started a war when he took Halleigh, so his intentions were to put a hole in Malek's head after he handed over the money anyway. He had to stay on his A game because he'd vowed to himself that he would never be caught slipping again. Especially not by Malek.

After a few more minutes of shooting off a string of ex-pletives to himself, hoping this was all just a nightmare, that Keesha hadn't been so stupid, and that he'd wake up from it any moment, Mitch realized that it was all too real. Deciding that he wasn't getting anywhere by sitting around thinking about the situation, Mitch got up and headed over to his spot on Seneca Street. He needed to drop off his re-up money. He also had the money that he owed to his connect with him.

Mitch called his sister on her cell phone and let her know he was on his way. He'd always made this particular run solo, never wanting anybody to know where he kept the mother lode at.

Mitch pulled up to the small brick house and hopped out with the bag full of money. He entered the house through the back and walked in. Hearing the sounds of the running money machines, he instantly got mad. His sister was slacking. He'd instructed her to have all the money counted up a week ago.

Mitch regretted paying her beforehand. He whispered to himself, "That's why I should have paid her after she was done." He entered the room, and the smell of the purple Kush graced the air. His sister and two of her friends were wrapping the one-dollar bills into rubber bands, passing the blunt around.

"I hate these damn ones," one of the girls said.

"You scared the shit outta me!" Ree took a deep tug of the blunt.

"What the fuck is going on? I thought I told you to have the money counted up days ago?"

Ree removed the blunt from her mouth. "Damn, bro! Relax." Ree exhaled and a ring of smoke floated from between her lips as she spoke. "You had so many damn ones in this batch! If you stop letting muthufuckas break into they kids' piggy banks to pay your ass, we'd get done a lot faster."

Mitch's two cousins chuckled.

Ree wasn't about to let him blow her high with his attitude. "But don't get your boxers in a bunch," she added, brushing Mitch off. "We are almost done." She smiled.

"Well, I got some more. I need it all counted up tonight. I have to go see Fredro this weekend, and I need to know where I am as far as the count. Got it?" He walked over to her and pecked her on the cheek. When it came down to business, he stayed hard on his sister, but he loved her more than anything and would do whatever to protect her.

"Got it, bro." Ree grabbed the duffel bag from his hands.

Mitch, a whole lot on his mind, left the house, not even acknowledging his cousins.

Chapter Ten

Malek and Scratch had on black masks as they tied up the three girls who they'd caught off guard inside Mitch's stash house. The girls never saw them coming as they crept in through an unlocked window in the back of the house. For Mitch to be as strategic and on point as he was in the game, Malek had anticipated more of a challenge. He thought for sure Mitch would have his main spot on better lock than that.

Both Malek and Scratch had scoped out the house, looking for any signs of cameras or whatnot. When they didn't notice any, they almost assumed that Grady had misled them. No way would anybody of Mitch's stature, with all the money he was making, not at least have cameras. Little did they know, Mitch purposely didn't have any cameras set at his stash spot, thinking that cameras would be a dead giveaway to someone who was trying to stick him for his paper. So, he made a business decision to try to make the house appear inconspicuous, as though it was just another house in the neighborhood.

Once Scratch and Malek had made their way into the unlocked window, they caught the ladies slipping with ease, engaging in the latest street gossip, smoking blunts, and counting money. Now Scratch held them at gunpoint, while Malek ran upstairs to where Grady said the money would be.

"In and out, youngblood!" Scratch yelled out to Malek, reminding him about robbing etiquette.

Scratch had schooled Malek to stay focused in a robbery. "Don't let your eyes and your mind wander onto anything else that might be of value or worth taking," Scratch had told him. "Greed is the surest way to fuck up a robbery. If you plan on knocking somebody over the head and taking their wallet, do just that. Don't get distracted by that shiny gold necklace hanging around their neck or that watch on the wrist. Take what you set out to take and keep it moving. It's always that last split second that can fuck a nigga up."

Following his own advice, Scratch stayed focused on the girls, who were trying to get out of their restraints. He told them, "Just stay calm and let us do what we came to do. Don't try screaming or anything, and it will all be over before you know it."

They did what he said, but he could tell by the look of fear in their eyes that they had doubts about making it out of the situation alive. "Look, baby girls, we ain't here to hurt nobody, so relax," Scratch coaxed the women. "I'm pretty good at tying knots, so I don't think you can wiggle yourself out of them there ropes. So just relax, baby," Scratch said smoothly, as if he weren't pointing a gun at them.

"Do you know who the fuck you robbing? Huh?" one of the girls spat, not able to keep her mouth shut, even though Scratch was standing there with a gun to her head. "You are a dead man walking. You're not even going to get a chance to enjoy that money, nigga!"

Scratch figured that was Mitch's sister, Ree. Her mouth alone was indication enough. She seemed to be the oldest of the trio and had braids straight to the back and a gold tooth in her mouth. Obviously she was ringleader of the girls, as she was the only one who decided to be hard-headed and get to running her mouth.

"And you can pull off that damn mask, *Scratch*. I know that damn walk and voice!" Ree yelled.

"Whatever you say, baby." Scratch glanced upstairs and wondered if Malek had found the money yet. "You all right up there, youngblood?"

Just as the words escaped Scratch's mouth, Malek came running down the stairs, skipping two steps at a time and carrying a duffel bag almost too full to even zip up. Bills fell out of the side of it. Scratch smiled. They had hit the jackpot.

"Yeah, I got it. Let's bounce!" Malek rushed toward the back door, followed closely by Scratch.

Scratch knew he wasn't playing the game right, being a halfway crook. The girls they were leaving tied up should have been dead, because they knew exactly who he was.

Back in his day, Scratch would have smoked them without hesitation, but he couldn't bring himself to kill the young girls, so he headed out with Malek, knowing everything he'd just participated in was going to come back to haunt him, probably tenfold.

Just before Malek and Scratch reached the back door, a loud gunshot erupted, startling Malek. He looked back and saw Scratch's eyes get buck and his lips shiver.

"Scratch!" Malek said, a confused look on his face. He was no longer confused when all of a sudden he saw blood seeping through Scratch's chest.

Scratch had taken buckshots to the back, and tiny holes began to appear through the thin material of his shirt as the tiny bullet fragments tore through his insides. Scratch's face told of his excruciating pain, and he fell into Malek's arms.

Shortly after that, another shot rang out. *BOOM!*

Malek ducked and moved Scratch to the side as he went for his gun. He had no idea where the shots were coming from. For a split second he thought maybe Mitch or someone had run up into the house, but it wasn't long before he realized that the loudmouth girl had freed herself.

Ree was now blasting at him with a shotgun that had been hidden under the couch. The petite girl tried her best to hold the large firearm and point it at Malek. She was relentless, and it was obvious she was going for blood, trying to take his head off.

Malek quickly fired two shots into the girl's abdomen, and she dropped instantly and yelled out from the burning heat of her wounds.

"Aghh!" she screamed.

Malek silenced her with another shot, this time to the head. Blood began to seep out of her mouth. Malek ran over to her and kicked the shotgun away from her body. He could hear the other two girls crying in horror as they'd just witnessed their girl shot to death.

Malek looked down at the body of the dead girl and shook his head. "Why did you have to do that?" he asked her, almost in a pleading tone. Like Scratch, the last thing he wanted to do was to kill any of those girls. All he wanted was the money, and now, because of her trying to play Rambo, two people were dead.

He looked back over to Scratch, who was lying on the ground in a puddle of his own blood. Malek rushed over to his side and picked him up. "Hang in there, Scratch. I'm going to get you to a hospital. Everything's going to be all right."

Malek knew he was telling Scratch a lie, giving him false hope, but he couldn't bring himself to tell him he would never make it. Nor could he just leave him there to die without even trying to get him help, not as long as he still had life in him. Scratch had become more than an accomplice in all of the madness. He was a friend who loved Halleigh. And because of that, Malek would always have endearment in his heart for Scratch.

Before Malek could even carry Scratch to the door, Scratch began to choke on his own blood, and his body began to tremble. Although dying, he still managed to unleash his infamous smile.

Scratch stared into Malek's eyes. "Youn-youngblood, I

haven't felt this alive in years. You made this old man feel young again." Scratch, his life slipping away, took a swallow of his own blood and gripped Malek's arm. "You made Scratch feel important. Didn't even look down on me. You let me ride shotgun with you, baby boy . . . like a gangster, ya know. I haven't ridden in a front seat of a car in years," Scratch said, reflecting on his life as a junkie. "I was yo' potna." Scratch gasped and then began to shake even more. He still continued to smile, though he knew his life was ending. He could feel his body temperature dropping as a cold chill took over his body. Not even Malek's words could give him any hope now.

"Yeah, that's right, Scratch. You my mu'fuckin' partner." Malek's eyes began to water, but no tears fell. It was hard to look at Scratch dying, but he tried to remain strong.

Scratch said in almost a whisper, "Go get my baby girl and get her home safe. Hear me? Tell her that I'm sorry for everything and that I never got a chance to tell her, but . . . I'm . . ." Then his voice trailed off.

"I'ma get her, Scratch. Just stop talking, man. Save your energy." Malek nodded his head up and down.

Malek felt Scratch release his grip and watched the old man take his last breath then look away aimlessly. Malek shook Scratch and called his name, but it was too late. He was gone. Malek closed Scratch's eyes and whispered, "I'll tell her how much you loved her, fam. I'll tell her how much you helped." With those last words, Malek kneeled down and laid Scratch's lifeless body on the ground and folded his arms over his chest.

Malek rose to his feet and left, leaving the other two

girls tied up and alive. The same thoughts Scratch himself had had just moments ago about knowing better than leaving eyewitnesses alive crossed Malek's mind as he headed out. But too many people had already been hurt behind the bullshit, and Malek wasn't going to contribute to the death of yet another individual, unless it was Mitch or anyone standing beside him. But the two girls' lives he would spare.

Making his way back to his ride, Malek knew he needed to go somewhere and get his head together. Plus, he would have to change his clothes to avoid suspicion, because he was covered in blood. He stopped at Hallwood Plaza and went into Champs to get himself some sweat pants, a clean T-shirt, and a hoodie. He then headed across town to check into a nearby hotel. He needed to get his head together and calm himself before he went to see Mitch. With or without the half-million dollars, he was going to get Halleigh.

Chapter Eleven

Tasha sat on the hotel bed counting the money she had taken from the stash spot, while Halleigh took a shower behind the closed bathroom door. They had agreed to split the money down the middle, so that each of them could have a chance at making an exit out of the city. But Tasha figured that she was entitled to that little bit of extra paper for putting her ass on the line to help Halleigh in the first place. She hurriedly stashed a stack of bills into her bag before Halleigh got out.

She heard the shower stop and then zipped up the duffel bag and sat across the room from it. Halleigh came out of the bathroom, her body wrapped in a towel. Tasha put her hand on her mouth as she looked at Halleigh's pregnant stomach. She was still small, but her slightly protruding stomach was a clear indication that she was with child.

Tasha gave Halleigh a half-smile. "Wow, you're really about to be somebody's mother, huh?"

"Yeah, I know, right?" Halleigh replied with a slight laugh. "I still can't believe it myself." She looked down at her stomach. "I don't do that well taking care of me. How in the hell am I going to take care of a baby?"

Though Halleigh tried to make light of the situation, Tasha knew her concern was real. Tasha was skeptical of Halleigh's mothering skills because she knew how truly weak Halleigh was without Malek. Never the type of woman to go out and accomplish things on her own, Halleigh had always depended on someone else. It was almost like she had banked on being Malek's NBA trophy wife, and when those dreams fell through, she was left on stuck. She went from depending on Malek to Manolo to Mimi to finally depending on Tasha. It was a never-ending cycle of bull-shit. Tasha couldn't believe that after all these years, after all Halleigh had been through, she still wasn't self-sufficient or independent. Tasha shook her head in disbelief and sent a quick prayer up to God for Halleigh's child.

With a soft-ass father like Malek and a lost soul like Halleigh for a mother, that baby is going to be all fucked in the game, she thought. "Are you ready for all of that?" Tasha asked.

"Is anybody? I know I'm young, but I can't see myself not having this baby. Malek and I are always drifting in and out of each other's lives. This was one thing that fate couldn't change. I'll always have a piece of him with me through this baby. This baby is Malek and me. I'm scared as hell, but I know it's going to be worth it."

"Are you sure, Halleigh?" Tasha asked again, just for good measure.

"Yeah, I said I'm sure!" Halleigh screamed back, becoming agitated by Tasha's doubt.

"Okay, okay." Tasha could see that her line of questioning was getting to Halleigh, so she changed the subject. "Are you okay? You might want to go to the hospital to make sure your baby is okay. Did they do anything to you?"

"I'm fine, Tasha. Mitch brought a doctor over to check on me and make sure I was okay. Right now I'm just trying to find Malek. I have to get to him before something bad happens. I just have a gut feeling that something isn't right with him. I tried to call him three times when we first got here, but his phone went straight to voicemail," she said in a worried tone. "Have you heard anything? I mean, you must have heard something. How did you know where to find me, or that I was even being held hostage in the first place?"

"I haven't heard anything. I haven't really been in the mix like that either. I knew about what happened to you because Keesha was at the club putting your shit all out in the streets, bragging about how Mitch had taken you."

"The club? What were you doing at the club?"

Tasha didn't speak. She just put her head down, ashamed that her life seemed to be a never-ending cycle of bullshit too. Seemed as though both Halleigh and her had come full circle.

"You're back at the club?" Halleigh asked, surprised,

reading the expression on Tasha's face. That was the last place she expected Tasha to return to, and the one place Tasha had vowed she never would. *But, hey, shit happens. Life happens.*

"What? Everybody can't live the high life like you and Malek, Halleigh! Any chance I had of being happy Malek took away from me when he killed my brother. Just like he is all you have, Maury was all I had. So, yeah, I'm back at the club." Tasha shook her head in disgust. "Damn it, Halleigh! You have no idea. You live in this shallow little Malek bubble. You need to wake up. That boy ain't a fucking saint. You and him sit up on a high horse and look down on the rest of the city like you're gods. That's why Mitch took you, Halleigh, because of him. And that's why he is in so much shit."

"I don't care what he did to anybody else. I only know how he treats me. I have to find him." Halleigh rubbed her stomach. "For both of us."

Halleigh could hardly sleep. The next day, she was going to go back to their home, even though Tasha didn't think it was a good idea. Halleigh couldn't wait. All that night, she lay restlessly as she thought of Malek, praying over and over in her head, *God, please keep him safe.*

Halleigh didn't know if Mitch's threats were real, but she wouldn't put anything past him. One minute he was talking sweet in her ear, all the while disrespecting Malek, who was supposedly his business partner and friend. The next minute, he was snatching her from her peaceful home and turning her world upside down. She knew that the only person she could ever trust one hundred percent was Malek.

Not even her own mother had been worthy of it or had earned it. She knew Sharina was the real problem in it all. She had started a cycle of hurt and pain for Halleigh.

Halleigh desperately wanted off the roller-coaster ride of violence and drama, but there seemed to be no way out. Tears came to her eyes as she thought of her predicament. Everything she had done in her past was now affecting her present and would undoubtedly affect her future.

I'm a fucking mess, she thought. *My life is like a bad soap opera.* Her silent tears transformed to audible anguish. She hoped that Tasha was asleep and couldn't hear her muffled cries.

Halleigh knew that Tasha disliked Malek, and as bad as she wished she could repair her and Tasha's friendship, as long as she stayed focused on Malek, that wouldn't happen. Still, Halleigh had to make the effort. Tasha had saved her, after all.

Besides that, Halleigh really did have love for Tasha, who had helped her through so many hard times, although frankly, those were times she'd rather forget. She couldn't change the circumstances under which they met. *She was Manolo's bottom bitch. Her job was to keep me there,* Halleigh thought. She couldn't help but think that if Mimi and Tasha had been up front with her in the first place about what she was getting herself into when they took her in, she would have never chosen to stay with Manolo and gotten sucked into his web of manipulation and fear. There was no doubt in Halleigh's mind that she and Tasha would have never crossed paths if she had never gotten caught up in the streets.

Over the years, Halleigh had become a product of the hood, but deep down on the inside, she wasn't built like Tasha. They were not the same type of women, never had been, and Halleigh was just now realizing that. *What type of woman would want to see another woman go through what I did? Was she ever really my friend? Yeah, she helped me kick heroin, but she was one of the many reasons why I felt like I needed the drug in the first place. Tash is my girl, but Malek is my man. He has never done me dirty. He's overlooked all of my flaws just to be with me, and he doesn't look down on me. He's the only person I've ever cared about that hasn't disappointed me, so if I have to make the choice, it will always be him.*

Chapter Twelve

Malek sat in his hotel room and counted the money, which was scattered all over the bed. He looked at his bloodstained clothes and kept seeing visions of Scratch struggling for his life just before taking his last breath. Although Scratch was older and an ex-fiend, he had courage, and Malek respected and admired Scratch's heart. He was loyal to Halleigh and the reason Malek had gotten enough money to get his woman back from Mitch.

Once Malek finished counting, he realized he'd gotten just over what he owed for the ransom. He loaded up the big duffel bag with a half-million dollars and headed to see Mitch. Something in his stomach told him things were going to end badly for everyone involved. There didn't seem to be a winner in any of it. At the end, even if he got Halleigh back and was left standing, he would still be in trouble. It seemed like he was going from one problem to the next without any resolution.

He exited the room with the money and headed over to Mitch's trap spot to make the switch, exhaustion plaguing his body and mind. He tried to push the thought out of his mind that Mitch, after realizing he'd been involved in the robbery of his stash spot and the murder of his sister, would retaliate by killing Halleigh.

As Malek drove through the city streets, his mind was not on vengeance, but it was on his entire life's struggles. Feeling defeated, he took a deep breath and hoped to God Mitch hadn't got wind of the robberies. He had to move quickly and get Halleigh before Mitch found out.

Once he arrived at his destination, he hopped out of his car, duffel bags full of money in hand. He approached the trap house that Mitch told him he would be at. As Malek approached the row house, he took a deep breath. Two young guns who once worked under Malek stood guard at the door. They couldn't have been any older than fifteen or sixteen.

When Malek approached, they couldn't even look him in the eyes. They just looked past him and opened the door for him to enter. Malek looked at each boy in the face and made sure they felt his animosity. If they ever crossed paths again under any circumstances, he couldn't be held responsible for his actions.

Malek slid past them and entered the house, which was full of hustlers. It seemed like Mitch had called all of Flint in to witness the drop-off. Once again, Mitch was determined to prove to everybody that he was the boss.

Malek's showing up let Mitch know that he had no idea Halleigh had escaped. Now he really felt on top of the world. Mitch wanted the whole organization to see Malek broke-down. He smiled as he saw Malek enter. "Check him," Mitch ordered as he stood from the table he was sitting at.

Three henchmen ran up on Malek and began to search him. Malek clenched his jaws as he lifted his arms, the bag still clutched tightly in his hands.

"He's clean," one of the men said as they walked away from him.

"You got my money?" Mitch gave Malek a menacing smile.

"Yeah, I got it," Malek said aloud, but in his mind he thought, *I got your money literally, nigga.* He dropped the bag and kicked it toward Mitch. "It's all there. Now, where is Halleigh?" Malek demanded through his clenched teeth.

Mitch unzipped the bag and flipped through the money. "Damn, my nigga! You actually got the money, huh—a fucking half a million dollars in just a few days. You must really love that bitch."

Malek wanted to lunge at Mitch for the disrespectful comment, but he had to hold his tongue and keep his cool, at least until he had Halleigh back in his possession. But after that, no telling. The joke would be on Mitch anyway, once he found out he was getting paid with his own money. He took a couple of deep breaths. "Where is Halleigh?"

Mitch remained silent as he flipped through the money and took his time before answering Malek. "Where is Halleigh?" Mitch asked himself out loud, trying to be sarcastic. "She might be at a spot on the South Side, or maybe she's inside one of my spots in the projects." Mitch lit a cigar filled with weed.

Malek's fist involuntarily balled up, and he was heaving, his chest going up and down. His temperature was rising, and he wouldn't be able to contain himself much longer. Mitch was trying to play him, and he didn't have the patience to play games, not after all he'd been through.

"Look at this nigga . . . about to cry like a little bitch!" Mitch said.

The whole room burst into laughter at the comment, except for Malek, Halleigh's safety being the only thing on his mind at that point.

Laugh now, cry later, Malek thought as he anticipated getting his girl back and then going after Mitch for revenge. He hated leaving his gun inside his car, but he knew Mitch's boys would have patted him down and taken it from him.

Mitch walked over to Malek and stood eye to eye with him. He was so close, their toes were touching. It was an intense, silent moment as the two men stared each other down. What had once been love between brothers was now hatred. Mitch's jealousy had led them to this point. Neither of them had any sign of retreat in their eyes.

Mitch was the first to move. He pulled out an all-black .45 and raised it to Malek's face. "Open yo' mouth," he ordered and then rested the barrel on Malek's lips.

Malek tightened his lips, looking Mitch in the eyes.

"If you want to see Halleigh again, you should do as I ask. Now, let me try this again. Open yo' mouth!" Mitch yelled.

Malek's pride was diminishing by the second, but the shame was worth Halleigh's life. He reluctantly opened his mouth.

Mitch jammed his gun inside. "I'ma only say this once—Flint is mine! I advise you get as far away from here as you can. You are dead in Flint. Dead! Jamaica Joe is not here to watch over your soft ass anymore; remember that. I can touch anybody in this mu'fuckin' city; believe that. Now, get the fuck out of my face!" Mitch struck Malek in the temple with the butt of his gun.

Malek dropped to one knee and cradled his throbbing face, blood trickling down.

Mitch stood over him smiling. He loved seeing Malek on his knees; it was pure satisfaction for him. He tossed a piece of paper it at him with the address Halleigh was being held at, as if to say, "Go fetch," even though Halleigh was no longer there. In fact, he was surprised that Malek showed up at all. He was sure the first thing Halleigh would have done was find her way back to him, but since she didn't, he decided to have a little fun. He was sending Malek on a wild goose chase, just for the hell of it.

He can find the bitch on his own time, but he can still pay me this paper for his disrespect. Mitch truly had the big head regarding his reign. He was the king of the city, and every man in the city needed to respect it.

Malek picked up the paper and hurried out, maneuvering through Mitch's goons to get out the door. He just wanted to go get his woman. He prayed to God that she was alive and well at the given location. He would deal with his beef with Mitch later, because he knew just as soon as Mitch discovered the real, it was gonna be war for real. All this other stuff would be a chick fight compared to what would go down between the two.

When Malek finally got to the house, he didn't know what to expect on the inside, All he knew was, he wasn't leaving out without Halleigh. He kicked in the front door, and the sound of cracking wood echoed throughout the stash house. He peeked inside the house, his gun in hand, and saw a man shot dead lying on the ground. The living room was in shambles, with overturned furniture and glass from shattered lamps everywhere. Even the TV had been knocked out of the entertainment case. It was obvious that there had been a struggle. His first thought was the struggle involved Halleigh. He just hoped to God she'd been victorious, and was thankful it wasn't her body lying there dead.

Malek immediately panicked. Scanning the room, he noticed the small monitor that displayed another area of the house. He stepped over the man and rushed to the monitor. He examined the screen and saw an empty room with a bed inside. The window had bars on it, and the sheets on the bed were wrinkled. He ran through the house calling out Halleigh's name, desperation evident in his voice.

"Halleigh! Halleigh! Where are you?" he repeated loudly as he continued to rummage through the house. He saw the stairs that led to the basement and immediately shot off the lock and opened the door. He yelled Halleigh's name as he ran down the stairs, hoping to hear his woman's voice at some point.

He reached the basement and looked around and saw nothing. His eyes focused on the bloodstained mattress, and his heart dropped at the sight. He fell to his knees and assumed the worst. "Halleigh!" he yelled as tears began to pour down his face. A hollow feeling in his chest overcame him as he crawled over to the bed. He knew that was Halleigh's blood. He cried his eyes out as he thought about his woman and unborn child.

But his sadness quickly became fury toward Mitch. "Muthafucka!" he yelled. He stood up and began punching the air as if he was punching Mitch in the face. "Son of a bitch knew Halleigh wasn't here and did this to torture me. He killed my baby." Malek broke down again, dropping to his knees on the mattress.

After a couple of minutes, he stood to his feet and, almost in a daze, walked up stairs, his head hanging low. He was a man possessed, and the only thing on his mind was murder. He was going to make any and everybody involved pay. As a matter of fact, he didn't care if they weren't involved. Anybody who had anything to do with Mitch or Sweets was as good as dead, just like his family.

Knowing the drug game, he was sure Halleigh was in the trunk of somebody's car, or in a dumpster somewhere. Every time he thought about her lying dead, it was like a dart to the heart. *This nigga made me go through all of this.*

He made me do all of this when he knew he was going to kill her.
I should've known. I should've protected her.

He slowly walked up the stairs, and the first sight he saw was the man lying on the floor. Out of anger, he loaded another bullet in his body for good measure. As tears rolled down his cheek, he exited the stash house on a path of revenge.

Chapter Thirteen

Mitch couldn't believe the news he had just received as he spoke on his cell phone with his cousin, one of the two girls Malek and Scratch had left breathing. He yelled to his goons as he held the cell phone up to his ear, "Everybody get the fuck out!" He watched as everyone exited the house. No one asked what was wrong, knowing what was best for them. He took a deep breath and placed his phone back to his ear. After swallowing hard and trying to maintain his composure, he said into the phone, "What the fuck you mean? She can't be dead," his voice cracking slightly.

She was telling him that his sister Ree was shot dead by a robber, and that one of the robbers was also lying dead in the house.

"I didn't recognize either one of them," she cried. "But I heard Ree say something about recognizing his voice and calling him *Scratch, Itch,* or something like that. But the other one got away, right after he shot Ree."

At that moment, Mitch knew exactly who the robber that got away was. He knew Malek was responsible for his sister's death.

Just then, something else dawned on Mitch. He looked down at the duffel bag full of bills and realized that he had been paid with his own drug money. "Fuck!" he yelled as he hurled the bag to the floor in frustration. Here he was laughing at Malek, when in actuality Malek was having the last laugh.

Mitch closed his cell phone without saying another word. Tears streaming down his face, he picked up the bag and headed out the back door to where he always parked his car.

On his way out he called his other sister, who was in their hometown of Saginaw, to break the awful news to her. His sister Toy, Ree's twin, was in a league of her own. You couldn't mention her name if murder wasn't in the same sentence. Mitch was distraught as he waited for his only remaining sister to pick up the line. When she didn't answer, he flipped down his phone and rushed to the car, so he could head to his house.

Mitch was sick to his stomach, and his hands shook violently. His sister had been his responsibility, and because of his resentment toward Malek, she had been murdered. He never in a million years wanted her to get caught in the crossfire of his and Malek's beef. He imagined that's how Malek felt about Halleigh, but at least Halleigh was still alive.

How did he even know where my stash house was? Mitch asked himself. *I was careful. I know I was careful. When I find out who let that shit out of their mouths, it's a wrap.*

His emotions, an equal blend of grief mixed with hate for Malek, were getting the better of him. He instantly regretted letting Halleigh and Malek live, and wished that he'd put a bullet in Malek's head when he dropped the money off.

Mitch was so busy putting his phone away, he didn't see Malek creeping from around his car with a gun. Before Mitch could even react, he was staring down the barrel of Malek's pistol.

Mitch had no fear, because Malek was just the person he wanted to see. Tears still on his face, he dropped the bag and intensely stared at Malek.

"Where in the fuck is Halleigh?" Malek asked.

Mitch smiled sadistically. "I sent her to the same place you sent my sister, mu'fucka!" he lied. He knew his words would incite retaliation from Malek, but at that point, Mitch didn't care. The only thing he knew was, his sister was dead, and Malek was the cause of it.

Malek pulled back the hammer on his gun. "We had a deal, you dirty mu'fucka."

"You killed my own flesh and blood. Your bitch is dead. Did you think I could let your people live after what you did to mine, you stupid muthafucka? Did you think I was gon' let your bitch live, with you trying to pay me her ransom with my own fuckin' money?"

Mitch knew that his words weren't true, but it was obvious that Malek didn't know that. He said it just to get under his skin. It was his only way to get a little bit revenge before he went out. There was no turning back. Too much had gone down between the two of them. Someone had to die. And from the looks of the scene at hand, Malek had the upper hand, so Mitch knew his seconds were numbered.

"You were supposed to be my nigga. I put you on."

Mitch responded with a smirk. He hawked up some spit and sprayed it right in the direction of Malek's face.

Malek immediately moved his head to the side, just missing the mouthful of mucus.

Mitch then reached for his gun on his waistline, but before he could even grip his pistol, Malek fired three rounds into his chest.

With Mitch confirming that Halleigh was dead, a sadness Malek had never felt overtook him. As the bullets left Malek's gun, it was like therapy for him. He was tasting a full serving of revenge. He watched as Mitch's body fell to the ground and blood poured out of his chest, painting his shirt crimson. Malek stood over him and fired three more rounds, rocking him to sleep forever.

When Malek heard the distant voices of Mitch's goons as they came running from the front of the building, he grabbed the bag full of money and hurried over the fence onto the next block, where his car was parked.

Chapter Fourteen

Halleigh and Tasha sat in the motel room, uncomfortable with each other's presence. There was a lot of tension between the pair of old friends, and there seemed to be a huge elephant in the room. Halleigh couldn't help but wonder why Tasha had come for her at all, if that's the way she truly felt about her. After reuniting with Malek and turning her back on her, Halleigh was surprised that Tasha was willing to put her life on the line for her.

"Thank you, Tasha," Halleigh said. "I really appreciate what you did for me. I thought I was going to die in there."

Tasha didn't respond. In her eyes, Halleigh's gratitude was long overdue. She remained silent while Halleigh continued to speak.

"I'm sorry, Tasha, for deserting you when you needed me most. I'm sorry about what happened to Maury." Halleigh genuinely was sorry about Maury's fate. She'd really gotten close and had gotten to know him. Just as it was with everyone else in Halleigh's life, it seemed Malek was the only thing that stood between her and Maury eventually getting even closer.

"You just won't admit that Malek killed him, will you?" Tasha asked, emotion in her voice. "The man you love killed my brother, Hal. How am I supposed to know you didn't help set that shit up? I trusted you. I loved you like a sister, girl." Tasha looked Halleigh in her eyes. "And even more so, Maury loved you. I can only imagine how you treat people who don't give a shit about you."

"Tasha, I'm not going to lie to you. I had a lot of love for Maury. He made me feel special after Manolo had stomped me into the dirt and had my self-esteem at an all-time low. Maybe in another lifetime we could have had something good, but I couldn't fully invest in him, Tash, because Malek had the keys to my heart. Maury was a good guy, Tasha, and I feel so bad about what happened to him. I've never asked Malek about what happened that night, because a part of me doesn't want to know. I can, though, tell you that I didn't have anything to do with it." Halleigh paused for a moment in an attempt to try to read Tasha.

When Tasha gave her nothing, she went on. "Don't you find it a little ironic that Mimi died that same night? That was my girl too, and I loved her. But you know she was grimy. Did you ever think for one moment that whatever went down she might have had something to do with it and not me? I cared about your brother, and I love Malek, even if he is the man that killed him."

"That's fucked up." Tasha shook her head from side to

side, unable to accept a half-ass apology. "You were my girl, Hal. Then you just forgot about me."

"Is that what you think? That I forgot about you?" Halleigh let out a chuckle. "You were the sister I never had. I love you so much, Tasha, and I am so thankful to have had you when I was going through all of the bullshit, but think about it. It's hard to get your man to understand that you used to be a ho. I used to trick myself out to some of the same niggas that be in Malek's face, Tasha. Think about how that makes my man feel. He doesn't have anything against you personally, but he didn't want me around the bullshit anymore. To tell you the truth, I didn't want to remember that life. I was running from it too."

"If you forget your past, you are bound to repeat it, Halleigh. I can understand where you coming from, but if I was on the same fake shit as you, then I would have left you in that house and never looked back. I guess me and you arc just two different types of people. If you're my girl, then that's it. There ain't a nigga in the world that can pull me away from you. I'm loyal, but that's not something that everybody respects. It's cool, though. I'm not tripping on it. Now I just know where we stand."

"Tasha, we will always have each other to lean on. You know if you ever really needed something and I had it, I would give it to you in a heartbeat," Halleigh said with a slight smile.

Tasha nodded and wiped a lone tear away. She knew Halleigh well enough to know she was being sincere and meant every word she was speaking. "Same here, Hal," Tasha said. "Just so you know . . . I forgive you."

"Thank you. That really means a lot to me," Halleigh replied and then initiated a hug between the two.

"Okay, enough of that mushy stuff," Tasha said, breaking contact. "Have you heard anything from Malek yet?"

"No, I keep leaving him messages. Every time I call, it goes straight to voicemail. I've left him like ten messages. I left him a message on his voicemail telling him where we're at, but he just won't call me back. I'm so worried about him. I don't know what I will do if something happens to him. I'm about to have his baby. I can't survive without him."

"You better learn how to, Halleigh, because even if he lives through this shit right here, in the lifestyle he's living, there will be other times like this. You've got to think about your baby. Even if you do it alone, you've got to do it. You already knew this was one of the consequences of dating someone in the game."

"But that's just the thing," Halleigh said. "He's not in the game anymore. He got out."

Tasha let out a laugh. "That's what they all say, Hal, that's what they all say. But even so, tomorrow ain't promised to no man. You still need to learn how to be independent and do things on your own."

"I don't know if I can."

Tasha could see that her words were getting to Halleigh, so she turned on the TV to change the mood. Even though she did not believe what she was about to say, she let the words come out of her mouth anyway. "Malek is a trooper, so you know he's all right, girl. We just have to find him, so he can get you out of town. Everything is going to be all right." Tasha scooted toward Halleigh and comforted her. She didn't want her to suffer alone.

"I know, I know. That's what I want to believe, Tasha, but something isn't"—Halleigh stopped mid-sentence as she saw a picture of Malek on the eleven o'clock news. "Tasha, turn that up."

Tasha obliged, and they listened to the news reporter.

"Former Flint Central High School basketball star was involved in a bank robbery. Here is a clip of him, along with another unidentified man, robbing Chase Bank and First National Bank early yesterday morning. Flint police officer, Robert Snell, was killed at the scene, and this incident has the entire police department on a manhunt.

"Police have yet to release any further details about the robbery, but surveillance video has confirmed the identity of one of the robbers as Malek Johnson. This is not Mr. Johnson's first time being involved in armed robbery. A few years ago he was charged and arrested for holding up a corner convenience store just months before he was expected to be drafted into the NBA.

"Authorities do not want the community to underestimate this suspect. He is armed and dangerous, and if you see this man, you should call the police department immediately. If you have any idea of the whereabouts of these men, please call 1-800-CRIMESTOPPERS. This is Anari Simpson, signing off from Channel Seven News."

Halleigh's mouth practically hit the floor when she saw a picture of her man on the screen. They had used an old high-school picture and put his face on prime-time TV. Halleigh knew that somehow, just like last time, she was the cause of his extreme measure. She could just feel it that her being held in that basement had something to do with Malek robbing those banks. Tears began to fall as she put her hands on her mouth and remained silent.

Tasha was also shocked as she looked along with her. Tasha didn't think that Malek had it in him to stick up a bank, let alone two. But obviously she was wrong. She had thought all of his balls came from the backing of Jamaica Joe.

I guess he's got a little bit of gangster in him after all, Tasha thought as she still sat in shock.

Halleigh began to hyperventilate and was becoming short-winded.

Tasha placed her hand on Halleigh's back, trying to help her. "Are you okay?"

"I just need some cold water," Halleigh said as she placed her hand on her chest.

Tasha jumped up and ran into the bathroom to run Halleigh some water. "It's not getting that cold." She opened the door and went to the ice machine outside, leaving Halleigh in the room alone.

Chapter Fifteen

Malek couldn't believe what he was seeing on the TV. He watched as his high-school basketball picture appeared on the television screen. He shook his head as his heart began to beat fast. He had to get out of town, and quick. A part of him wanted to believe in his heart that Halleigh was alive, but he knew she was gone. Mitch's words wouldn't let him think otherwise.

Initially, Malek wasn't sure that the police officer he'd shot was dead, but the evening newscast confirmed it. He buried his face in his hands and began to cry. His life had fallen to pieces, and he had nothing. No Halleigh, no child, and no love. The drug game had consumed him and swallowed him whole. He wished he had chosen another path in life, but in actuality, he didn't choose the game, the game chose him.

The guilt of Halleigh's and his baby's death was on his heart. He gripped his gun and put it to his head. He had nothing else to live for. Not even the money was worth living for. His eyes became bloodshot red, and his hand shook as he held the gun to his temple. He believed he was responsible for Halleigh's death, and the pressure was too much for him to bear.

Everything in the room was blocked out, and the only thing Malek could hear was the sound of himself breathing, as flashbacks of him and Halleigh making love in the islands appeared in his thoughts. He saw her pretty smile. The thought of never seeing it again was breaking his heart.

He quickly pulled the gun away from his head and tossed it on the hotel's bed. He couldn't bring himself to take his own life. That would be the easy way out. Malek's mother had always tried to teach him the right way was God's way. He didn't want to burn eternally for committing suicide, although he wasn't so sure that he'd go to heaven anyway, because of all the wrong he had done.

He stood up and began to pace the room back and forth. He had a bag full of money and didn't know what to do next. It seemed like every move he made was a bad move, so now he was just stuck and indecisive.

Afraid, confused, misguided, and alone, at that moment Malek realized he needed Halleigh. At first he thought she needed him, but without her, he had no purpose. The universal pull of soul mates was inevitable, but Halleigh had been pulled to a place where Malek couldn't follow. *Then how come I can still feel you, ma? It's like you're somewhere out there calling for me. I can feel your heart, Hal,* he thought as fresh tears came to his eyes.

He kept thinking about Halleigh's body lying somewhere and rotting. That thought alone was driving him crazy. He knew he had to get out of the room and make a run for it, but what then? Where would he go? Who would he turn to? Malek didn't have a clue, but he did have a bag full of untraceable dirty money, and that always did the trick. He would have to go far away and begin anew. Start a new life and try to move on from the chaos, death, and destruction. *I'll always carry you with me, Hal. There will never be another woman for me. You're mine, and I'm yours . . . in life and in death.*

Malek snapped out of his love funk and began to think of how to get out of town. He couldn't stay in the same spot for too long for fear of being apprehended. The entire police force was probably searching for him at that very moment. *I've got to get the hell outta dodge.*

He had checked in the hotel room under his name, just to get off the streets, and knew it would only be a matter of time before the cops found out where he was hiding. At first, he didn't care if the cops found him; that's just how messed up in the head he was. But now he was coming to his senses.

Malek's thoughts seemed to be disorganized and jumbled, though. It was the worst way to be when devising a plan. Scatterbrains made bad decisions and didn't think things through fully, but Malek's nerves were too bad to even consider that.

He gathered the bag of money and his gun and headed outside so that he could start his car so it could warm up in the brutal Michigan winter weather. Just as he walked out, he saw what he thought was a familiar face brush by with a fur coat on. She pulled up her collar, trying to block the cold winds, but that prevented him from getting a good look at her. He was glad. He didn't need anyone spotting him, especially her, if it was in fact who he thought it was.

"Malek!" he heard someone call out.

Malek didn't pay the voice any mind as he continued his trek to his car parked toward the back of the parking lot.

"Malek!" she yelled again, her hands on her hips. "I've got Halleigh!"

At first he just looked around suspiciously as he made his way to his vehicle, but when he heard those last words come out of her mouth, he stopped immediately and turned around, hope entering his body.

Tasha couldn't believe the man she was looking for was right in her face. *What a coincidence*, Tasha thought at first, but then she remembered someone once telling her that there are no such things as coincidences. *Maybe, just maybe, this Halleigh and Malek thing was meant to be.*

"What did you just say?" he asked urgently as he began to head back toward Tasha. He was so wrapped up in what Tasha had just said, he didn't even notice the cop cars heading toward him.

"I said I have Halleigh," Tasha repeated. "She has been trying to call you. She's called like forty times. Haven't you gotten her messages?"

Malek patted his pockets to retrieve his phone, but felt nothing but empty space. He couldn't imagine where his phone had gone as he tried to recall where he was when he recalled having it last. *That muthafucking junkie.* Malek remembered Grady giving him a hug. "Where is she?" he asked Tasha, not pressed about the cell phone.

"She is in the hotel room going crazy over you. You have to go help her," Tasha said. Then she saw flashing lights whip into the parking lot just a few hundred feet away from them.

The police cars went around the building, giving Malek only a matter of time to make a decision on what to do. Malek couldn't believe what he had just heard. Tasha's statement gave him hope, but it was short-lived. Malek, at that point, didn't care if he got caught by the police. The only thing he was thinking about was his woman and if she was really alive, because for a split second, he wondered if Tasha was setting him up, trying to lure him into the hotel room so she could get some type of reward money for his capture or something. But it was a chance he was willing to take.

Malek rushed toward Tasha with the bag in his hand. "Where is she? Where is she?" he yelled as he neared her. "Tasha, look, I don't have a lot of time. Take me to her." He grabbed Tasha by the shoulders and looked around to see if the cops had made their way back around.

"She's in the room," Tasha said, hurrying toward the motel room that Halleigh was in. Malek followed, holding the bag full of money.

* * *

When Malek got to the motel room with Tasha, he saw Halleigh sitting on the bed, gripping a blanket. When their eyes met, it was as if a magnet had drawn them together. Halleigh rushed over to him and grabbed him, squeezing him as tight as she could as tears began to flow freely.

Malek slightly lifted Halleigh off her feet and hugged her tightly as he buried his face in her neck, smelling her scent. "I have been going crazy trying to get you back." He looked into her eyes. "Did he hurt you?" Malek quickly thought about what she could have possibly been through. "Did Mitch hurt you?"

Halleigh looked into Malek's eyes and saw a look of deep concern accompanied by defeat.

Malek clenched his jaw tightly and gently placed his hand on Halleigh's stomach as he awaited her answer. Halleigh could see that Malek was blaming himself for what had happened to her, and she didn't want to bring him more pain. She wanted to tell him what they had done to her and tell him everything that she had been through, but she couldn't bring herself to add more stress to Malek's plate.

"No, Malek, I'm fine. I'm okay, baby. Don't worry about me. I missed you so much. I was so afraid that I was going to lose you, Malek," Halleigh said, refusing to let Malek go as she felt the tension and stress melt away from her body. Malek was like her savior, and as long as he was near her, everything in her world was all right.

Tasha rolled her eyes at the sight. It almost made her

want to vomit, but somewhere deep inside herself she wished that she could know a love so pure and true as the one before her.

Malek kissed Halleigh passionately and got on his knees to speak to his unborn child.

"The baby is okay," Halleigh said, reassuring him as he wrapped his arms around her waist while still kneeling on the floor.

"Daddy's here now. I'm never going to let anything happen to you again. I put that on everything I love," he whispered to the baby.

Before Malek could say anything else, Tasha interrupted him. She was looking out of the window. "Police are everywhere!" she said as she looked on in amazement. Tasha quickly regretted helping Halleigh. She didn't sign up for any police trouble, and the last thing she needed was a case for aiding and abetting.

"Fuck!" Malek rushed to Tasha's side and peeked out of the window.

Five police cars were spread throughout the vicinity. They seemed to have the entire hotel on lock. The flashing lights intimidated him. He was clearly outnumbered. "They must've seen me come in." Malek's mind began to race. The Flint Police Department was gunning for his head for killing one of their own.

"Is what they're saying about you on the news true?" Halleigh asked Malek, hoping he would tell her something different. Malek remained quiet, and his silence was her answer.

Malek took out his gun, walked over to Halleigh, and kissed her like it would be his last time ever doing it.

Halleigh felt it and wasn't having it. "Whatever you are about to do, I'm doing it with you," Halleigh insisted without a drop of fear in her heart.

At that very moment, she reminded Malek of Scratch and how set he'd been on having Malek's back. "No! Just know that I love you." Malek gave her another hug and kiss. He was about to go out blazing with the cops because he knew they weren't planning on bringing him in breathing.

"I have an idea." Halleigh grabbed his hand.

Tasha looked on in disbelief, waiting to see what was to unfold.

Toy looked at the body of her dead brother Mitch as the paramedics put a white sheet over his body. She was infuriated and thirsty for revenge. With her long-braided cornrows and loose jumpsuit, she looked like one of the boys as she was surrounded by her goons from Saginaw. She had just gone to identify the body of her twin sister, and wasn't expecting to come bury her brother along with her.

Sweets walked up on her, and Toy's goons immediately reached for their guns.

Sweets put up his hands to signal there wasn't any beef. "Slow down. I'm Sweets. Mitch was my man. We did business together."

"I know who you are. You the faggot, right?" Toy said,

hiding her green eyes behind the Dolce & Gabbana glasses that sat on her face.

Sweets clenched his jaws at her comment, not because she called him a faggot, but she was being blatantly disrespectful. He gave her a pass, since she had just lost two of her loved ones. "Yeah, I'm the faggot," he answered sarcastically. He rubbed the front row of his teeth with his tongue.

"Set up a meeting," Toy said. "I want to talk to his crew ASAP."

Toy was a boss in her own right. She moved heavy heroin in the Saginaw area, and actually, she was homosexual also. Mitch had given her the rundown on Sweets months ago. She knew they'd been doing business together, but at this point, until she got to the bottom of the situation, everybody was suspect.

Toy watched the paramedics cart off her only brother. "Do you know who is responsible for this?"

Sweets slowly nodded his head and rubbed his hands together slowly. "Malek."

As soon as the name came out of his mouth, Toy knew exactly who he was talking about. Mitch had also talked to her about Malek when he and Malek were hustling together. At first when he told her about his new business partner, he sounded confident and happy, as if he had found his long-lost brother. Slowly, over time, his conversations regarding Malek began to change, and Mitch would tell her of Malek's arrogance and inability to lead his troops. Toy knew it was only a matter of time before Mitch took

Malek's empire for himself, but she wasn't prepared for the young gun to come back with so much force, leaving her without her brother and sister.

Toy's trigger finger began to itch as she prepared to light the city of Flint up on behalf of her slaughtered family. "Set up the meeting!" she yelled, rage and pain in her voice. Then she walked off, her entourage right behind her.

Chapter Sixteen

Halleigh put on an Oscar-worthy performance, scream-ing as if she were scared to death.

"I will shoot this bitch!" Malek yelled. "Back the fuck up!" He pressed the gun to Halleigh's temple.

Malek inched his way to his car as at least ten police officers, partially hidden behind car doors, pointed their weapons toward Malek.

"Back the fuck up!" Malek jerked Halleigh closer to him. "Sorry," he whispered in her ear, trying to comfort her because he had her in an uncomfortable hold. "We almost to the car, baby."

Malek and Halleigh finally reached the driver's door, and Malek, with his free hand, opened it and stuffed Halleigh in. She scooted over, and Malek hopped in right after her.

The police officers tried to get a good aim, but Malek's

tinted windows hindered them, and they didn't want to risk shooting the innocent hostage by just blindly shooting at the vehicle.

Malek sped out of the parking lot with a trail of local police officers and state troopers on his tail.

Tasha remained back at the hotel room, tied up with sheets. Just in case the police questioned her, she'd appear as though she were a victim too.

Halleigh glanced back and saw the many flashing red, white, and blue lights. "Oh my God, Malek, they're on us!"

Malek hated that he had brought Halleigh along with him, but she had refused to let him go by himself and devising the hostage plan.

Halleigh saw the look in Malek's eyes as he pushed his whip just over ninety miles an hour on Pierson Road, trying to reach the highway. Lucky for him, Flint was not the type of city that harbored traffic jams. Mostly everyone in the city was broke and unemployed, so the streets were never packed with after-work cars. He floated through the few vehicles on the road as if he were an Indy 500 driver.

The longer he drove and shook the police, the more police cars seemed to accumulate behind them.

"Oh, shit, Malek. It's like twenty cars behind us!" Halleigh yelled out. "You've got to go. Drive faster!"

Malek, disregarding all traffic laws, was going as fast as the car would take him. He barreled through intersections, knocking other cars out of his way, holding Halleigh back against the seat with one arm, trying to keep her from getting hurt. "Put your seat belt on, ma!" he screamed.

"I'm with you!" Halleigh braced herself against the door handle as he swerved through traffic. She was affirming that she was willing to ride or die with her man.

Malek gave her a forced smile and gripped the steering wheel tighter. This wasn't the way he envisioned life with Halleigh. If it was his time to go, then so be it. He was a man and he had gotten himself into the situation, but he wanted Halleigh to die an old woman. He wanted her to see things and go places he'd only dreamed of. He wanted her to live and breathe. He wanted her to love and be free. Only after she experienced all these things did he want her to die; not right now. She hadn't done enough yet. In fact, she hadn't done any of it yet.

"I love you," Malek said.

"I love you too."

They jumped on the highway, police cars tailing them and spinning out of control as they turned onto the ramp without even touching the brakes.

Malek looked up and saw a news helicopter hovering just above them. They had managed to outrun the cops on the highway headed toward Detroit. The police cars began to fall back as if on command. Malek figured that for some reason they'd deemed the chase too dangerous to pursue, but he couldn't outrun the aircraft.

Malek had a souped-up car. His Benz engine was custom-made to outrun any car in the police department. But he didn't think there was a car invented that could outrun a helicopter.

They were approaching the tunnel that ran between

Detroit and Canada. "I know they're going to have tire spikes to stop us after the tunnel," Malek said, sweat dripping from his forehead. He had watched too many high-speed chases on television to be green to their tactics. Even though they were crossing into Canada, he had no doubt they'd be stopped.

Malek looked over to Halleigh to see how she was doing, only to find her peeking over his shoulder like she was the lookout chick. Halleigh didn't care what happened, just as long as she was with Malek.

They entered the tunnel doing at least 130 miles per hour. Malek knew they only had about a minute or so before more cops got on them to catch them after flattening their tires. He stopped in the tunnel and threw the car into park.

Halleigh looked at him like he was insane. "What are you doing?"

Malek took a couple deep breaths and then looked at her. "I love you, Halleigh. I always have. You are the only person I got in this world. I want you to know that you are my soul mate."

"I love you too, Malek. You all I got too. Why are you talking like this is the end?" Halleigh tried to figure out what Malek was about to do.

"It is." Malek's eyes began to water, but he remained strong as he displayed his smile, trying to put Halleigh at ease.

They could hear the police sirens nearing the tunnel exit. Malek knew it was time to go through with his final plan.

"Let the baby know that I loved him or her, okay?"

"*Loved?*" Halleigh said, trying to understand why he was talking in past tense as if he was preparing to die.

"Look, Jamaica Joe used to use this tunnel to bring drugs in from across the border, so I know another way out. There's an old escape hatch that I'm gonna take you to. I'll distract the cops to give you some time to get out the tunnel." He handed her the duffel bag full of money. "Take this and go to a bus station. Get the hell out of Flint for good. I want you to never look back. Understand?" Malek cupped her face and stared deep into her eyes.

"No, Malek, I am not leaving you. We're in this together. It's me and you against the world, remember?"

"Halleigh, go! We don't have much time." Malek revved up the engine.

Halleigh shook her head in defiance. "I'm staying with you."

Malek couldn't change her mind. He took a deep breath and prepared for what he was about to do. He gripped her hand tightly. "No one loves you more than me, Hal."

Chapter Seventeen

Every local channel was covering the breaking story of Malek taking a hostage on a high-speed chase with the law.

Sweets and the Shottah Boyz were sitting in his living room, waiting for Toy to arrive. "Can you believe this shit?" Sweets asked as he watched Malek on television.

Sweets didn't want to admit it, but he was kind of glad that Mitch was dead. He was finally in total control of the city. *The North Side crew took each other out. Dumb niggas! It's my time now,* he thought silently as his crew watched the chase like it was an action movie.

One of Sweets' goons, who was glued to the television, said, "The camera lost him in the tunnel."

Everyone waited in anticipation as the news helicopter filmed the police officers waiting on the other end of the tunnel so that the road spikes could slow Malek down; but Malek's car didn't come out.

"They're gonna kill that mu'fucka as soon as he come out of that tunnel." Sweets laughed. "Ain't no way out. He either got to come out, or in a minute, they gonna go in there after his ass."

After about two minutes of waiting, Malek's Benz appeared, speeding wildly out of the tunnel. The car ran over the spikes, causing it to lose control and spin before it hit a railing and flipped repeatedly. Malek's car caught fire. Seconds later, the car exploded, causing a balloon-like flame to mushroom into the air.

A smile spread across Sweets' face as he imagined Malek burning to his death.

The news reporter was giving the viewers a play by play of the chaos, informing them that the chase had come to a tragic end. Seeing Malek's life crumble on television, all of the people in the house were smiling with satisfaction.

A knock at the door put a brief halt to their entertainment. Everyone reached for their guns, but Sweets told them to relax and put away their weapons. Mitch's sister was supposed to come and meet with them, so it was probably her.

"I hope this dike bitch don't think she's coming to fill her brother's spot," Sweets said. He had heard Mitch talk about her as if she was a street legend. From what Mitch told him, Toy had schooled him in the game. Mitch had also told Sweets that his sister was not to be underestimated. She was just as deadly as any killer walking the streets. Sweets didn't know what to expect, but he would soon discover what Toy was all about.

One of the Shottah Boyz answered the door and let Toy and her people in.

Sweets stood up to greet Toy as she walked in with four men. Toy left her signature shades on as she walked into the room like she owned the place.

"Toy, these are the Shottah Boyz. They worked under your brother." Sweets threw his head in the direction of the couch, where they sat watching the news telecast. "That's Malek, the dude you don't have to worry about anymore." He nodded to the television. "Looks like he's burning in hell." Sweets chuckled.

Toy wasn't at all relieved. She still wanted to know what went down between her dead brother and his now dead killer. "What went down between that rat bastard and my brother?" she asked Sweets.

"Mitch had Malek's girl kidnapped and wanted a ransom. But everything went wrong. I don't know how all of this shit happened. Mitch was here one minute, gone the next. Feel me?"

"Who was supposed to have my brother's back when he got killed? Who was with him?" Toy asked coldly, not wanting to hear anything extra come out of Sweets' mouth.

Sweets looked at the Shottah Boyz, who were supposed to always have Mitch's back, and Toy's goon wasted no time loading up all three boys with bullets. Sweets was taken by surprise as he watched the young boys he had practically raised die from multiple gunshots.

Toy pulled out her gun and put it to Sweets' neck. She put her lips close to his ear. "Now that that's taken care of, who killed my family?"

In shock, Sweets couldn't fix his lips to say anything. He just stared at the boys as their eyes were rolling in the backs of their heads.

"Who is responsible?" Toy was ready to put her murder game down and take out all of the city of Flint to get to the bottom of things.

"What the fuck?" Sweets became frantic. He wanted to reach for the gun in his waist, but five people had their guns trained on him at that point. Sweets felt his knees get weak as his entire team had just been murdered. "Why did you have to do that?" Sweets asked, almost in a pleading tone. He looked at his young'uns, and his heart broke in two. "That nigga Malek killed him. Malek did it, bitch!" He pointed to the TV screen.

The room was silent, except for the voice of the news reporter. Malek's face appeared on the screen.

"This is a picture of Malek Johnson in his better years, when he was a superstar high school basketball player headed for the pros. Now this once promising life has come to a tragic end. . . ."

Toy asked, "That's him?"

Sweets nodded his head as he clenched his fists. He wanted to kill Toy, but was in no situation to act on his impulse.

Toy sent a single shot through Sweets' skull, reuniting him with his crew.

What Malek and Jamaica Joe had spent years trying to

accomplish, she had come to town and done in literally days. She had killed the infamous Sweets. Her main focus now was getting revenge for the death of her family members. She didn't care if Malek was dead. She wanted every trace of Malek Johnson wiped from the planet. She wouldn't rest until she saw everyone who had ever associated with him suffer and die.

Toy wiped Sweets' blood from her face. "Check the house and see what they got in here," Toy said. She was an opportunist, the exact kind Scratch had spoken of. She didn't want to leave any money in the house. Toy was a hustler first, killer second.

They stumbled upon the surveillance tape that Sweets had just retrieved from the stash house where Halleigh had been held captive. Toy and her crew examined the tape and saw a woman pacing back and forth in a room, looking scared. It didn't take them long to figure out that this was Malck's girl, the one Sweets had said was being held by Mitch. Hate flooded Toy's heart. The way she saw it, this bitch was part of the reason her brother was dead.

They kept watching, and witnessed the moment when Tasha broke into the room and rescued Halleigh.

"Who the fuck is that?" Toy asked. But it didn't really matter who the other woman was. Toy knew it wouldn't take her long on the streets to ID this chick, and then she'd be dead. If she rescued Malek's woman, then Toy considered her an enemy. Anything and everyone connected to Malek or Halleigh was living on borrowed time.

Toy and her crew grabbed the tape and headed out, itching to kill.

Chapter Eighteen

Sharina lay in her hospital bed, looking at the newscast and hoping that her baby was okay. She saw Malek's face on the television and listened as they described him as a ruthless, cold-blooded killer. They also kept showing video footage of Malek and an unknown robber sticking up a couple of banks. When Sharina saw the footage, she automatically knew it was Scratch. A small smile spread across her face as she watched Scratch do his infamous walk into the bank.

"Scratch ain't gon' ever change," she said to herself. Her smile quickly faded when her daughter's face appeared on the screen and the news reporter said she wasn't a hostage, but an accomplice on the run with Malek.

Sharina began to pray for her baby. She wished that Halleigh could see her clean and sober. She didn't want to be remembered as a junkie and bad mother. Once she finished her silent prayer, she thought about how she'd never told Halleigh who her real father was.

Back in 1984, Scratch had fathered her after a one-night stand. At the time, Sharina was dealing with another man, who was doing better financially than Scratch. She decided to go with that man because she thought he had a better future. How could she tell Halleigh that her father was a junkie and bum that stayed on the streets?

The man Halleigh believed to be her father died when she was five. He was a good man, so Sharina thought it would have been selfish to let Halleigh find out that he wasn't her father.

Sharina saw the door crack open and noticed an unfamiliar face. The woman had long braids and didn't seem to be a nurse.

Without saying anything, the woman walked toward Sharina, and the look in her eyes expressed pure hatred. The woman slowly closed the door and smiled at Sharina, but the smile wasn't a warming one. It was more like a sinister smirk.

Sharina could see the devil in the woman's eyes, and her fear filled the air.

The woman pulled out a gun with a silencer from her waistband and pointed it at Sharina. She took her time, so she could be precise and accurate.

Sharina froze in terror. Before she could reach for the nurse's call button, a hollow-tip bullet went through her skull, killing her on contact, splattering blood on the white bedsheets.

Toy held the gun and smiled. Her vengeance rampage

had begun. She would not rest until she felt she'd erased every last memory of Halleigh and Malek from the city. They had stripped her of the only family she had, and now everyone was going to pay. Flint had never experienced a killer like Toy, but they were about to get put on game.

Tasha had nothing to complain about. She had the money she took from Mitch, and no police troubles. She had managed to free herself from the sheets and slipped out of the hotel room while the police gave chase to Malek and Halleigh.

Later, she discovered that everyone from the old crew was dead, even Sweets.

"Karma is a bitch." She smiled and licked her thumbs as she sifted through the bills. She thought about Halleigh, but those thoughts were short-lived. She was gonna worry about herself and herself only.

Tasha was so busy counting the money, she didn't notice the person creeping up behind her.

Toy and her crew had broken into the back of the house. Flint was small, so it wasn't hard for Toy to find out who was the woman in the video and then find out where she lived.

When Tasha felt someone was in the room with her, it was too late. Toy had an all-black TEC-9 pointed to the back of her head.

"Oh my God," Tasha whispered, taken by surprise.

"God can't save you now, baby girl," Toy said in a low tone, admiring Tasha's pretty hair.

"I came to talk to you about Halleigh." Toy pulled up a

seat in front of Tasha, who was still in shock. Before she killed her, Toy had a few questions for this beautiful woman. The details were still sketchy, but talk on the street let Toy know that this chick was close to Halleigh. She probably had inside information that would help Toy understand exactly what happened to her brother.

Tasha didn't know the woman that sat in front of her, but she wasn't going to ask who she was either. "Please don't hurt me," Tasha said in a pleading tone. Her eyes never left the gun Toy was holding.

Toy smirked and then stroked her hand down Tasha's soft hair. She looked deep into Tasha's eyes, almost mesmerized by her beauty. Although she was about to kill her, she took a liking to Tasha. "You and me have some things to talk about. If you tell me what I want to know, maybe I'll make your death quick and painless."

A tear ran down Tasha's face. Her whole body was trembling.

"I'll even put this gun down while we talk," Toy said as she leaned back in her chair. She kept the gun pointed at Tasha, but put it down in her lap. "So, let's start at the beginning. Tell me how the fuck my brother Mitch let himself get killed by this muthafucka Malek."

Chapter Nineteen

One Year Later

Baltimore, Maryland had a different feel, a different vibe, and different people. It was a long way from Flint, Michigan, but Halleigh and Malek were happy. They were living in a quiet area just off the east side of B-more, far away from Flint's ills and their police. They had a new-born baby boy, and life seemed to be going good.

After Halleigh refused to escape from the Detroit tunnel without him, Malek had quickly devised another plan. Using a sand bag he had in his trunk, he placed it on the accelerator, causing his Mercedes to exit the tunnel at full speed. The resulting explosion was even better than Malek had hoped for. With the police and news helicopter crew distracted by the huge flames, Halleigh and Malek were able to get out of the tunnel undetected and make their

161

way to the bus station. No one was looking for them at this point, because everyone assumed they were both inside the burning car. It was weeks before investigators discovered that there were no human remains among the ashes recovered at the scene. By that time, Halleigh and Malek were living in Baltimore under new names, while the bewildered cops were still searching for them on the streets of Flint.

Malek used Mitch's money to buy a small brownstone, and invested the little he had left in a small coke operation. Malek didn't do it too big. He knew he had to make just enough money to get by and stay under the radar.

He thought for a minute about going legit, but he deemed it to be true what they say: The game pulls you in and never lets you go.

He watched Malek Jr. during the day while Halleigh went to her part-time job at a store at Mondawmin Mall. It worked out good, because the owner paid her off the books, so there was no record that she worked there. Malek had told her that was the only way she could work, since they couldn't risk being tracked down. Even though they were living under assumed names, Malek still didn't want to take any chances. Although he wasn't in Flint, he still suffered from paranoia, and was always on the lookout for anything out of place.

One night, Malek came in late from doing his thing on the streets, and found Halleigh asleep on the couch with Malek Jr. on her chest. Malek locked the door behind him and peeked through the window with his gun in hand.

When he was satisfied no one had followed him, he turned to look at his sleeping family.

He removed Malek Jr. from Halleigh's arms and held him to his chest. He got instant relief when he saw Halleigh's eyes slightly open up and a smile form on her face.

She then closed her eyes, the residue of the smile still on her face. It was something about her smile that made Malek feel warm inside. As long as he had that smile in his life, everything would be okay. If she was happy, he was happy.

He watched as the sun came up, and wondered what his life would have been like had he gone to college . . . if he had never gotten into the street life. What if Halleigh didn't have her innocence stripped from her?

All of these unanswered questions would remain that way, so Malek had to play the cards he was dealt. Those cards included a son he was proud of and vowed to do right by. He walked Malek Jr. into the bedroom to spend some time with him before putting him in his crib.

It was only a few minutes later that Halleigh woke up. She had been dreaming about Tasha, remembering the tight bond they shared during the years they worked together on the streets. Halleigh felt she owed her life to Tasha. If Tasha hadn't come to rescue her from Mitch's place, things could have turned out very different for Halleigh and Malek.

Although Malek had warned her to never make contact with anyone in Flint, Halleigh felt bad that she hadn't talked to Tasha. She felt like she at least owed it to her

Treasure Hernandez

friend to let her know that she had a baby boy. He might never have been born if it weren't for what Tasha had done.

Thinking about Tasha had become almost a daily thing lately for Halleigh, and after tonight's dream, she felt like it was a sign. It was time for her to talk to her friend.

She heard Malek's voice in the bedroom, playing with their son. She peeked into the room, and Malek didn't even notice her. Feeling it would be safe to make just one quick call, Halleigh walked into the basement, where Malek wouldn't be able to hear her. She dialed Tasha's number, hoping it hadn't changed.

She smiled when she heard Tasha's phone ring. It had been a year since she'd talked to her.

"I forgive you, Halleigh. I've moved on, and I'm glad to hear that you are doing good. I wish you well," Tasha said as she squirmed in her bed.

Moments later, without even saying bye, Tasha hung up and began to shake feverishly. She looked down at Toy, who was giving her the best oral sex ever. Toy worked her tongue like a professional and pleased Tasha better than any man had ever done. They had been lovers for about a year, and Toy had Tasha turned out and sprung on her.

Toy's pretty, wavy hair wasn't braided as it usually was, and with her clothes off, she was immaculate. Tasha watched as Toy pleased her, then moaned as she exploded all over Toy's face.

Toy came up and smiled, knowing she had just pleased

164

her woman. "Is that who I think it was?" She wiped Tasha's juices off her face.

"Yeah," Tasha said, running her fingers through Toy's hair.

Tasha had been with Toy ever since the day Toy had come to kill her. Toy always got what she wanted, and she wanted Tasha. Toy was blown away by Tasha's beauty, and gave her an offer she couldn't refuse: If she became Toy's girlfriend, she would live.

Tasha wasn't gay and never thought in a million years she would go that way. Initially she agreed only so she could stay alive, but Toy had the swagger of a hustler, and Tasha eventually fell for it.

Aside from the sex, Toy kept Tasha around because she was sure that someday she would lead her to Halleigh, who would no doubt lead her to Malek. When the police finally figured out that there were no bodies in the burned-up Mercedes, the hunt for Halleigh and Malek was all over the newspapers. Toy wasn't even pressed to look for them, because she was so certain that one day they would resurface, and then she could get her revenge. It looked like that day had finally come, and Toy couldn't be happier.

She picked up Tasha's cell phone and looked at the number, noticing it was a Baltimore number. Then she smiled and went back down on Tasha.

Epilogue

Halleigh sat at the front desk at the store typing into a laptop, since there were no customers. Ever since she'd called Tasha a couple of days earlier, she'd been feeling better. All of the loose ends were finally tied back home in Flint. Tasha had forgiven her for being with the man that killed her brother, so Halleigh was at peace with herself.

Halleigh began to get teary-eyed as she thought about all the things that had occurred in her life. She often wondered about how her mom was doing. Although her mother had been nothing short of a bad parent to her, she just wanted to know how she was. Halleigh thought about her life of prostitution, hustling, and stripping at the hands of the game.

She looked at the computer screen, proud of what she had accomplished. She had just penned a novel, and her hard work had finally paid off. "I'm all finished," she whispered.

She smiled and continued to reflect on her life. At the age of twenty-one, she had gone through more than most sixty-year-olds and lived to tell the story. That in itself was an achievement.

Halleigh scrolled to the first page and added the finishing touch to her book. It read: *This book is dedicated to good ol' Scratch. I know you're watching down on me. Love you.*

Halleigh closed her laptop, unaware that she had just dedicated her book to her father. She thought about Scratch's gap-toothed smile.

She was also unaware of someone standing in front of her at the counter until she looked up. "Whew! You scared me," Halleigh said. "I didn't see you come in. Can I help you find anything in particular today?" she asked the customer.

Halleigh looked at the butch female who stood in front of her. The woman wore dark designer glasses and long French braids to the back. "No, I don't need any help. I know exactly what I'm looking for."

Halleigh didn't understand what the woman meant by that statement, but she would soon find out.

Coming Soon

A Girl from Flint

Prologue

K arma is what put me in that hellhole. I don't even
know how I ended up in jail. A couple years ago I was
on top of the world. I've had more money flow through
my hands than most people ever see in their entire lives. I
was the woman that everybody wanted, and I had my way
with some of the richest men in the Midwest. From presti-
gious businessmen to the most hood-rich niggas in Flint,
I've had them all. We thought it was a game, and in a way
it was. We were trained to be the best. Skilled in the art of
seduction, we were professionals who knew how to please

in every sexual way. In my family, the mentality was, if you ain't fucking, you don't eat.

Growing up in the hood, I had to use what I had to get what I wanted. My pussy was my meal ticket, and in order to stay on top, I juiced every nigga green to the game. I felt like, if a dude was stupid enough to let me trick him out of his dough, then he deserved to get got. "Fuck me, pay me" was our motto, and I used to laugh when my girls would shout that after we hustled men out of their money.

It's not quite as funny these days, though. Now I've got a prison sentence hanging over my head, and I'm locked in this cage like an animal. I haven't washed my hair in months, and I'm looking over my shoulder every minute of every day, hoping these bitches in here won't try to get at me. I don't know, maybe it was my destiny. All the wrong that I've done, all that shit came back like a boomerang and hit me harder than I could have ever imagined. I sit in this jail cell every day wondering how I landed in a state prison, a maximum-security state prison at that.

When I heard the judge say those words, it brought tears to my eyes. It was like a nightmare about my worst fear, only I couldn't wake up. It was real, and there was no waking up from it.

My downfall was . . . well, you'll learn about that later.

From the very beginning of my life, I was headed in a downward spiral. My mother is a crack fiend, and I haven't seen or spoken to her in years. I never knew my father. He died before I got the chance to get to know him. I hear that he really loved me, but the fact that he wasn't in my life affected me. I never had that male figure in my life, and that pains me greatly.

As you read this novel, understand that this is what happened to me, and that everything that you do has its consequences. I remember we would talk about opening up our own salon and not needing a nigga to support us. That was before my life got complicated. Believe me, if I could turn back the hands of time, I would have never stepped foot in the murder capital—Flint, Michigan.

Yeah, that was the first of our mistakes. Honey made it seem so live, so wonderful. I thought it was the city that would make all my dreams come true. The truth of the matter is, everyone in that damn city has hidden agendas and is looking for a way to get paid, by any means necessary. I was a little girl trying to do big things in a small city. I should've just kept my ass in good ol' New York.

Me and my girls thought we were the shit. We got whatever we wanted, when we wanted it, from dick to pocketbooks, even first-class vacations around the world. We used men until their pockets ran out, and when we were done, we tossed them aside and moved along to the next. Some people may call us hoes, gold-diggers, or even high-paid prostitutes, but nah, it wasn't like that. It was our hustle, and trust me, it paid well. Very well.

I wish I could go back to the good ol' days when we used to smoke weed in Amra's room and open the windows so Ms. Pat wouldn't find out. Or the days when we used to lie about staying the night over each other's house so we could go to parties and stay out all night. Those are the memories that make this place bearable. Those are the times that I reflect on when I get depressed and when life seems unfair. The times when it was just me, Honey, Amra, and Mimi, the original Manolo Mamis.

There have been many after us, but none like us. All them other bitches are just watered-down versions of what we used to be. That's who we were; that was our clique. That's the friendship that I miss and think about when I feel lonely. The thought of how close we used to be is something I would cherish forever.

I know I'm rambling on and on about me and my girl-friends. You are probably wondering, *Bitch, how did you end up in jail?*

Damn, I'm so busy trying to tell y'all what happened, I forgot to introduce myself. I know y'all wanna read about Halleigh and Malek and all that high-school bullshit, but let me get my piece off first. I promise you, you won't be disappointed. I'm Tasha, and this is my Flint story.

Chapter One

As Lisa looked into the mirror, she could not recognize the eyes that stared back at her. Everything started running through her mind all at once. She thought about the loss of her only love, Ray, his death, and about their creation, Tasha. Tasha was the only positive thing in her life. Her bloodshot eyes stared into the mirror as she looked into her lifeless soul and began to cry.

Lisa tied a brown leather belt around her arm and began to slap her inner arm with two fingers, desperately searching for a vein. As the tears of guilt streamed down her face, she looked at the heroin-filled needle on the sink and reached for it. She hated that she had this terrible habit, but it called for her. She wasn't shooting up to get high anymore; she was doing it to feel better. She needed the drug. She tried to resist it, but the drug called out to her more and more. When she wasn't high, she was sick and in tremendous pain, and her body fiended for it.

She injected the dope into her vein and a warm sensation traveled up her arm. The tears seemed to stop instantly, and her frail body slowly slumped to the floor, her eyes staring up into space. All of Lisa's emotions and her negative thoughts slowly escaped her mind as she began to smirk. She could not shake this habit that a former boyfriend had introduced her to, and her weekend binges eventually became an addiction.

Her addiction affected her life, as well as her daughter's. All of her welfare checks sponsored the local dope man's chrome rims, ice, and pocket money. Her life started going downhill after the death of Raymond Parks, better known as Ray.

It was 1982, the era of pimping. Lisa was fifteen when she met Ray, who was twenty-one at the time and a known pimp in the area. Ray approached Lisa while she was walking to the store. He pulled up and slyly said, "Hey, sweetness. Wanna ride?"

Lisa paid him no mind and kept walking. She started switching her ass a little harder while walking, knowing she had an audience. She pretended not to be flattered by the older man and flipped her sandy-brown hair.

Ray parked his long Cadillac at the corner and stepped his shiny gators onto the streets of Queens. He took his time and eventually caught up with the thick young woman with hazel eyes. He slid in front of Lisa, blocking her path.

"Hello, beautiful. My name is Raymond, but my friends call me Ray. I wouldn't have forgiven myself if I didn't take the time out to meet you." Ray stuck out his hand and offered a handshake.

Lisa looked up and saw a tall, lean, brown-skinned young man. She couldn't stop her lips from spreading, and she unleashed her pretty smile. She shook his hand and said with a shaky voice, "I'm Lisa."

Raymond smiled and stared into her eyes. Lisa stared back, and her eyes couldn't seem to leave his. He knew he had her when he saw that all too familiar look in her eyes. He asked in a smooth, calm voice, "Can I take you out sometime?"

"My mama might not like that."

Ray smiled. "Just let me handle her. So, can I take you out sometime or what?"

Lisa blushed. "Yeah, I guess that'll be all right."

Raymond gave her his number and asked her how old she was. Lisa told him that she was only fifteen. Ray's facial expression dropped, disappointed to know she was so young. He didn't usually approach girls her age, but she had an adult body and was by far the most beautiful girl he'd ever seen. He grabbed her hand, looked at her, and told her to give him a call so he could pick her up later that day.

Lisa watched Ray get into his car and pull off. She couldn't stop smiling to herself as she continued to walk to the store. *He was a fly brother. I hope my mama let me go.* She hurried to the store so she could get home and call Ray. She knew that it would take a miracle for her to get her mother's approval, but as fine as Ray was, she was definitely going to try.

Lisa called Ray later that evening, and an hour later he was at her front door with a dozen roses in each hand.

Lisa's mother answered the door and was impressed by the well-dressed young man that stood before her. She noticed he wasn't around Lisa's age and became skeptical about letting him in.

Ray sensed the vibe and quickly worked his magic. He handed the flowers to her and took off his hat to show respect.

Ray didn't get to take Lisa out that night. He and Lisa's mother talked, and he charmed her for hours. He barely spoke to Lisa the entire evening. A professional at sweet-talking, he knew that to get Lisa, he had to get her mother first.

As the night came to an end, Ray said good-bye to Lisa's mother and asked if Lisa could walk him to his car. She agreed, and they exited the house.

Lisa and Ray stood in the driveway. He took her by the hand and said, "I never saw a lady so fly. I want you to be mine . . . eventually. What school do you go to?"

"McKinley."

Ray shook his head then said in a soft voice, "I know where that's at. I'll pick you up after school tomorrow, okay?"

Lisa started to cheese. "Really?"

He grabbed Lisa's head, kissed her forehead softly, and whispered, "See you tomorrow."

She turned around and entered her mother's house, and Ray took off as soon as he saw that she got in safely.

The next day, Ray was parked outside of the high school in his Cadillac waiting for his new "pretty young thang," as he called her.

When she got into the car, Ray smiled at her. "Hello, beautiful. How was your day?"

From that day on, Ray and Lisa were together. He took her on shopping sprees weekly, and she was happy with her man. He never asked for sex and never rushed or pressured her in any way. Lisa wondered why the subject never came up, and wondered if he was physically attracted to her.

Ray was very much attracted to her, but he'd promised himself he wouldn't touch her until she was eighteen. He had his hoes and women all over town, so sex was never an issue.

Lisa knew about his other women and his line of work, but never complained. Ray took care of her and treated her like a queen at all times. Over time, she fell deeply in love with him and never had a desire to mess with any other man.

Ray always made sure she had whatever she wanted and that she went to school every day. If she didn't do well in school, her gifts would stop, so Lisa became a very good student.

Occasionally Ray would help Lisa's mother with bills and put food in their refrigerator. Ray had money, real money. He was a pimp with hoes all over the city. He wasn't

the type to put his hands on a woman. He made excep-
tions for the hoes that played with his chips or disre-
spected him, but, in general, he had mind control over
many women, so violence was rarely needed.

Exactly one month after her eighteenth birthday, Lisa
found out she was pregnant with Ray's child. She couldn't
believe she had gotten knocked up on her first time, but
when she told Ray, he was the happiest man on earth. Lisa
dropped out of school, and Ray immediately moved her
from her mother's house and into his plush home in the
suburbs.

He used to put his head on Lisa's stomach every night
and tended to her every need. He promised that when he
saved up enough money, he would open a business and
exit the pimping game.

Eight months into her pregnancy, Lisa began to become jealous of Ray and all his women and confronted
him about it.

Ray reacted in a way that Lisa never saw. He raised his
voice and said, "Don't worry about me and my business!
You just have my baby girl and stand by yo' man!" He
stormed out of the house and slammed the front door.

Lisa felt bad for confronting him and began to cry. She
cried for hours because she'd upset the only man she ever
loved. Ray was all she knew. She stayed up and waited for
his return, but he never came.

That night Ray went around town to collect his money
from his workers. He was upset with himself for raising his

voice at Lisa. He'd never yelled at her before, so it was really bothering him.

He pulled his Cadillac onto York Avenue and saw one of his best workers talking with a heavyset man about to turn a trick. He thought to himself, *Make that cheddar, Candy.* He decided to wait until Candy finished her business before collecting from her. He sat back in his seat and turned the ignition off, listened to the smooth sounds of the Isley Brothers and slowly rocked his head.

He looked back at Candy and noticed that the man and Candy were entering a car parked on the opposite side of the street. Candy was his "bottom bitch." She always kept cash flowing and never took days off. He smiled. *Candy going to make that fool cum in thirty seconds.*

Suddenly he saw Candy jump out of the car, spitting and screaming at the man. She walked toward the sidewalk spitting. The man jumped out of the car and started to yell at Candy, and yelled even louder when Candy kept on walking.

At this point, Ray calmly stepped out of the car and began to head toward her. The man had gotten to Candy and began to grab her and was screaming at the top of his lungs. Ray approached the man from behind and grabbed him. "Relax, relax."

"Mind yo' fucking business, playa. This bitch is trying to juke me out of my money."

"Daddy Ray, he pissed in my mouth! He didn't say shit about pissing. I don't get down like that."

Before Ray could say anything, the man lunged at

Candy, slamming her head hard into the brick wall she was leaning on. Ray immediately grabbed the man by the neck and began to choke him. His fingers wrapped tightly around his neck, Ray whispered to him, "Never put your hands on my hoes. If I see you around here again, it's you and me, youngblood." Ray released the man, and he dropped to the ground, trying to catch his breath. Ray stood over the man and pulled out a money clip full of cash. "How much did you give her?"

"Forty. I gave her forty," the man said, rubbing his neck.

Ray peeled off two twenties and threw it at the man and told him to get the fuck out of his office. The man took the money and ran to his car and pulled off.

Ray then turned around to help Candy up. She was lying motionless. He quickly bent down to aid her and noticed she wasn't breathing. He started to shake her and call her name, "Candy! Candy!" He got no response.

He gave her mouth-to-mouth resuscitation, and she began to breathe lightly. He knew he had to get her to the hospital, but he didn't want to be the one to take her in. It would raise suspicion if a known pimp brought a half-dressed hooker in, barely breathing and battered. He decided to go in her purse to see if he could find a number for someone that she knew, to check her into the hospital.

As soon as he stuck his hand in her purse, he saw flashing lights and heard a man on a bullhorn telling him to put his hands up. Then another police car pulled up.

Ray stood up, both of his hands in the air.

One of the police officers ran to the girl and put his fingers on her neck. He shook his head. The policemen handcuffed Ray and began to read him his rights.

"Wait, man, you got this all wrong."

"Yeah, yeah." The cop led Ray to his police car.

Ray began to pull away from him. "Listen, I was helping her. I didn't—"

Another cop hit Ray over the head with a billy club. "You got caught red-handed robbing this young lady. People like you make me sick."

Ray was too dazed to say anything as the cops put him in the back of the police car. He knew it looked bad for him. He dropped his head and began to pray.

The prosecutor stood up to give his closing argument. He wiped his forehead with a handkerchief then slowly approached the jury. "The man sitting in that defendant chair is a man of no remorse. He killed a seventeen-year-old girl in cold blood. Imagine if that girl was your daughter, your sister, or a beloved neighborhood child." He paused for effect. He wanted to give the jury time to process what he'd just said.

He pointed his finger at Ray. "This man is a menace to society and deserves to be punished to the fullest extent of the law. All of the evidence points toward one man, and that man is sitting before us today. That man is Raymond Parks. Nothing can keep our communities safe from this tyrant except a life sentence. The only people who can make that happen are you, the people of the jury.

"Don't put another young girl in danger. Put him away

for the rest of his life. He was caught over his victim's dead body, rummaging through her purse looking for money. He drove this woman's skull against a brick wall so hard and so violently, her brain hemorrhaged, which ultimately led to her death. How cold-blooded is that? So the prosecution asks of you—no, we beg of you—to sentence this man to a lifetime in prison. Render a guilty verdict and bring justice back to the community. I rest my case." The prosecuting attorney turned and walked back to his seat, a smug grin on his face. He knew he'd just delivered a closing argument that would cripple the defense and win the trial.

Ray looked back at Lisa and her swollen belly and felt an agonizing pain in his heart. He might spend the rest of his life in jail for a crime he didn't commit. He felt tears well up in his eyes as he mouthed the words, *I love you,* to Lisa.

Lisa looked into Ray's eyes and began to cry. She knew that the chances were slim for him to get off. She gripped the bench she was sitting on. *Please, God, let them find him not guilty. Please . . . I need him,* she prayed as the jury deliberated in a private room.

Half an hour later, the jury returned to the courtroom with the verdict. An overweight old white man stood up and looked into Raymond's eyes and said, "We, the jury, find the defendant, Raymond J. Parks, guilty of murder in the second degree and guilty of strong-armed robbery."

Lisa screamed when the verdict was pronounced.

Ray dropped his head as the guards came over to escort him out of the courtroom. He looked at his attorney.

"That's it? You said you could beat this case. I'm innocent, man. I'm innocent."

His attorney looked at him, shrugged his shoulders, and gave a sly smile. "We'll file an appeal."

Ray knew that his chances of winning the appeal would be just as slim as his chances of winning the trial. He looked at Lisa as they carried him out of the courtroom. *I love you,* he mouthed again as the guards handcuffed him.

Lisa felt so much pain in her heart. She just stood there and watched her only love leave her life. Helpless, she didn't know what to do. Ray was going to prison, and there was nothing she could do to stop it from happening.

She was so distraught, she couldn't control herself. She felt her dress become soaked and thought she had peed on herself. She felt liquid run down her leg and then realized it wasn't urine. Her water had broken. "I'm going into labor," she screamed to Ray just as the guards took him from her sight.

Her mother told her to sit down and then called a guard over for help.

Later that evening, Tasha Parks was born. It was the worst day of Lisa's life. The love of her life had been convicted of murder, and ironically, their child was born on the same day.

Lisa was depressed for months and cried herself to sleep every night with her newborn baby in her arms.

Ray left behind a house and some money in the bank, so she supported herself and her daughter with that.

Lisa visited Ray as soon as they let her. He had grown a

beard, and walked to the table where a thick glass window separated them. She picked up the phone, and so did Ray. Ray did not have the same look in his eye that he used to have. The sparkle had diminished. Lisa desperately looked, trying to find a piece of the man she had fallen in love with, but it wasn't there. He had changed. There was no warm feeling in his eyes anymore, only coldness.

"How are you?" she asked, trying to be supportive.

Ray shook his head and smiled. "Don't worry about me. Just make sure you take care of our child. Lisa, I'm gon' be in here for a long time. I love you, and I want you to always remember that. I'll love you to the day I die."

Lisa noticed his hopeless vibe. It seemed as if he was telling her good-bye forever. "You're coming home, baby. Your lawyer is gon' file an appeal, and you're coming home."

Ray had to stop himself from becoming emotional. "That appeal is bullshit, baby. They are going to find me guilty, just like they did this time. That's if the judge even grants an appeal. Just remember, I love you, and don't let my baby girl grow up not knowing that I love her too."

Lisa looked at their daughter and then at Ray. "Tasha and I need you, Ray. You're all we got. We need you." She put her hand on the glass.

A single tear streamed down Ray's face. "Tasha? That's my baby girl's name? Make sure you tell her I love her. Every day, make sure that she knows that." He arose from his seat, kissed his fingers, and pressed them against the glass. He then began to walk out.

Lisa gripped the phone tightly and banged it against the glass, "No!" she screamed. "Ray, I love you! I love you!"

Ray walked back over to the glass and picked up the phone. "I love you, Lisa, but don't come here again. I don't want you or my daughter to see me in here. You deserve more. I love you." With those words, he headed to the cage that would be his home for the rest of his life.

A few weeks later, Lisa was breast-feeding Tasha when she received a phone call. She felt the floor spinning as she tried to understand the news from the other end. When she was sure she'd heard what the voice said, she dropped the phone and fell to her knees, her baby in the other arm. "No!" she screamed as she cried. Tasha was startled by her mother's roar and began to cry too.

Ray had been stabbed fifteen times in the chest by a fellow inmate.

Lisa sank into a deep depression and moved back home with her mother after Ray's death. She would go for weeks at a time without talking to anyone or even bathing. She blamed herself for Ray's death, believing he wouldn't have stormed out of the house if she hadn't confronted him that night. *He would have stayed home with me,* she often thought to herself.

Lisa, looking for the same love that Ray had shown her, began to let men manipulate her into doing what they pleased. Any man who dressed nice and approached her had a chance. It became a problem when her mother grew tired of caring for Tasha while Lisa ran the streets.

* * *

Four years after Ray's death, another death was about to hit Lisa—her mother's.

When Lisa's mother died, she finally felt the burden of being a mother. Tasha had grown so attached to her grandmother, she even thought she was her mother, calling her Mama, and Lisa by her first name.

Lisa met a man by the name of Glenn, a pimp in the neighborhood. He was in no way as successful as Ray, but Lisa was drawn to him. In some way, he reminded her of Ray.

Glenn introduced Lisa to weed. She liked the way it made her feel and began to smoke it so much, it didn't get her high anymore.

Then he introduced her to cocaine, telling her, "It makes you feel good." Lisa used to snort a little cocaine with Glenn, but that quickly grew old. Eventually she needed a new high, and Glenn provided that too. And so it was she got hooked on heroin.